THE DEV

'But you don't know me – you don't love me,'
Persepha protested when the magnetic Don
Diablo Ezreldo Ruy announced his intention
of marrying her. 'In Mexico, *señorita*, the
knowing and the loving come after marriage,'
he told her. But would they?

Books you will enjoy
by VIOLET WINSPEAR

THE NOBLE SAVAGE
The rich, appallingly snobbish Mrs. Amy du Mont
would have given almost anything to be admitted
to the company of the imposing Conde Estuardo
Santigardas de Reyes. But it was Mrs. du Mont's
quiet, shy little companion who interested the
Conde . . .

THE GIRL AT GOLDENHAWK
Jaine was accustomed always to take back place to
her aunt, a spoilt darling of the London stage, and
her glamorous cousin Laraine. As it seemed only
natural to *them* that Jaine should take on the difficult
task of explaining to Jaine's wealthy suitor that she
had changed her mind about the marriage, Jaine
nerved herself to meet the arrogant Pedro de Ros
Zanto. Was there a surprise in store?

PALACE OF THE POMEGRANATE
Life had not been an easy ride for Grace Wilde, and
she had every reason to be distrustful of men. Then,
in the Persian desert, she fell into the hands of
another man, Kharim Khan, who was different from
any other man she had met . . .

THE GLASS CASTLE
'Out in the East they say that the mind of a woman
is a jungle, and it is the one jungle in which a man
should never get lost.' That was the code by which
Edwin Trequair lived – or so he told Heron. Why
then did he ask her to marry him? Could Heron
ever understand such a strange, arrogant man?

THE DEVIL'S DARLING

by

VIOLET WINSPEAR

MILLS & BOON LIMITED
17–19 FOLEY STREET
LONDON W1A 1DR

First published 1975
This edition 1975

© Violet Winspear 1975

ISBN 0 263 71880 8

Made and Printed in Great Britain by
Cox & Wyman Ltd, London, Reading
and Fakenham

CHAPTER ONE

THE dress was perfect, as she knew it would be, for her very own Lucrezia had made it for her and there was hardly anything the Italian woman couldn't do with her clever hands. The colour was a kind of sunset flush so that the soft pallor of Persepha's skin had almost a transparent glow, and her hair was even more burnished, pale as the gold that rims the last white clouds drifting out of a summer's day. Her eyes in contrast were hazel-brown, so that little lights seemed to dance in them. Persepha was lovely, and adored by her guardian, and sheltered ... especially from men.

Yet tonight a man had got hold of her and was, with an insistence his laughter didn't quite match, urging her in the direction of the Gothic garden house surrounded by luscious pink rhododendrons.

'You are the last old-fashioned girl left on this earth,' Larry Condamine chided her. 'It's the done thing to dance and kiss, and now you've danced, and divinely I might add, you must show me that you can kiss with equal skill. I mean it, Sepha! A girl with your looks has to be born knowing how to love, otherwise the gods wouldn't have made you the way you are. Perfect, adorable – oh, come here!'

Grown impatient of the way she had eluded his lips as they came through the garden, Larry caught hold of her and forcibly held her, a shaft of moonlight making his eyes seem feverish as he gazed down at her face.

'God, yes, you're lovely!' He almost groaned the words. 'I wish to heaven I could afford you, but that darn guardian of yours will never let you go to any man who hasn't thousands a year to spend on you. I hate it – don't you? – the way Marcus Stonehill keeps you out of the clutches of young men while putting you on show for those rich, card-playing cronies he invites to Stonehill Mansion. You must know what everyone says, that he plans to hand you over to the highest bidder?'

Persepha felt the urgent young arms around her, and somewhere among the shrubs she heard a nightbird chirping; a lonely sound that caught her attention as the urgings and arguments of Larry Condamine couldn't. Yes, Persepha knew what everyone said about Marcus, and some of it was fact, and some of it fiction. He did plan a successful marriage for her, in the sense that her husband must have real money as opposed to what Marcus made by gambling with rich fools, as he called them. He had always looked after her, ever since her mother had died, and because Persepha knew how much he had adored Daisy Paget, her actress mother, she didn't quibble that he laid down certain rules of behaviour and expected her to abide by them. It was because he had cared so much for Daisy, who had married a poor actor and undermined her health in shabby theatres, that he treated her with an iron hand in a velvet glove, and Persepha would not have dreamed of struggling against that hand.

'You'd better not kiss me,' she said to Larry, as she felt his lips against her cheek, warm and seeking. 'Not unless you want Marcus's riding whip across your shoulders.'

At once the seeking lips came to a halt. Rumour had it that more than one impecunious suitor had limped away from the gates of Stonehill, and despite his ardour Larry Condamine was not prepared to suffer in vain.

'Do you reckon you could love me?' he asked. 'I'd be prepared to go off to Australia with the right girl. I've heard you can buy land out there for a few thousand pounds and I can wangle that much out of my grand-mother. She'd be pleased to pay me for settling down. Well, what do you say, Sepha? Is it on?'

'Is the moon up there made of green cheese?' Persepha drew out of his slackened arms, and the skirt of her dress made a rustling sound as she turned and began to saunter back towards the house where a large party had been in progress and to which she had been escorted by Marcus himself, for the owner of the big, brightly lit house was one of the numerous business men whom her guardian knew and with whom he dealt, mainly across a gaming table. Going into business himself would have bored Marcus to death. He preferred games of chance, and he reminded Persepha of a Regency Buck and a member of the Hellfire Club.

She smiled to herself as she heard Larry following sulk-ily in her wake. He was quite nice, but it wasn't really because he had no money that she chose to fend off his advances. If she had loved him she'd have gone off to Australia and defied even Marcus. But Persepha had an idea that she didn't care much for the emotion called love ... she had been taught too well by Marcus Stonehill that once you gave your heart away there was no recalling it. Once you allowed yourself to care deeply for another person you let yourself in for heartache more often than happiness.

She was the first to arrive in sight of the terraced house where the light of chandeliers flowed out from the big room where couples had danced ... her quick young eyes saw at once that something appeared to be wrong, for those couples were now standing in slightly scared groups and their voices were hushed, shocked, as if whatever had happened had been rather awful.

Persepha stood very still beneath the arching fronds of a willow tree and she felt the lurch of her heart as a tall figure came down the steps from the terrace, walking silently through the crowd like some kind of a bronze-skinned Indian, or a tawny tiger in human shape. That was how Persepha had thought of him the first time he had come to Stonehill; she had been introduced to him in the library, but when he had left she had kept out of his way, leaning over the gallery rail where it was shadowy and watching unseen as he departed, throwing a long shadow in the lamplight that Marcus had a preference for. Walking with that lithe, silent, dangerous grace that was utterly foreign.

The next day Marcus had told her that the man came from Mexico and was so unbelievably rich that he made English potentates seem like the bosses of cotton mills.

'What's his name?' she had asked, trying hard not to sound as if she were curious, but because the man had struck her as so unusual she couldn't help but wonder about him. Not that she had liked the look of him ... her guardian wasn't a soft man, but the tall stranger had looked ... pitiless.

And right now Don Diablo Ezreldo Ruy came towards her, cutting a dark stern path through the silent guests, and it seemed to Persepha that the nearer he came the blacker his eyes seemed to grow, and those words of the other day came tearing back into her mind.

'He has the look of a devil,' she had said to Marcus. 'His mother must have thought so when she first looked at him and gave him that name. Don Devil!'

Marcus had laughed in that sardonic, lazy way of his ... but there had been something in his eyes when he had looked at her, an intentness unrelated to amusement which had made her wonder just what his connection with the Spaniard could be.

'Did you play cards?' she had asked, and had strolled

8

about the library looking at those choice oddments which Marcus kept around him, and she had paused in front of Daisy's portrait and seen reflected there an image of herself.

'My dear ward,' Marcus always called her that when he was feeling extra fond of her, 'a man does not gamble with his master.'

'Your master?' she had echoed, looking at her guardian in sheerest amazement. 'You have no master!'

'Not even God or the Devil?' he had drawled.

Yes, the memory of that conversation was overwhelming in Persepha's mind as the tall Spaniard came so silently to her, there beneath the green willow, and with that foreign inclination of his head spoke other words that she would never forget.

'I regret, Miss Paget, that your guardian has been taken ill—'

'Then I must go to him,' she broke in.

'No.' A lean hand with a fearful promise of strength detained her in her headlong rush to the house. 'There is nothing that you can do, *señorita*. It was a stroke of the heart – swift, fatal. I am the emissary of death and there is no way to avoid breaking the harsh news to you who was closest to him. It is a consolation at least that the blow struck him swiftly, just as he laid down a superb hand of cards. I was watching and I saw his hand – he was smiling, Miss Paget.'

'Smiling?' she echoed, dazedly. 'Smiling as he died?'

'Yes, *señorita*. It can happen that way.'

'But – no – Marcus can't be dead!' She screamed out the words as the pain of their meaning stabbed right through her. 'He's all I have! All I care about! Marcus! Marcus!' She went to run again, like a cat in pain and terror, and swiftly the Don's lean hands caught her, lifted her, and carried her off into the night . . . or so it seemed,

9

for it was then that Persepha fainted with shock, and didn't awaken again for hours, and by then she was in her bed at Stonehill and Lucrezia was there at her side, caring for her.

'*Carissima*, you must accept and not fight what is a fact in this terrible way. The *signore* has gone to his rest and there he will be again with Mees Daisy. She was his only love, my heart, and now you must think of them together as they could not be here on earth.'

'But Lucrezia,' the girl trembled in the arms of her old Italian nurse, to whom she had been handed as a baby when the lovely Daisy Paget had died only a matter of days after giving birth to her, 'he seemed so himself as we drove to the party. He was in a good mood – I could always tell – as if he had brought off some gambling coup that very much pleased him. He didn't complain of feeling ill in any way. Not like that time in Florence when he was ill – oh, Crezia, is that when it began? Did he have heart trouble and kept it to himself? It would be his way, dear darling Marcus.'

'He wanted never to cause you any suffering, my heart,' crooned the Italian woman, the tears welling into her eyes set deeply in a network of lines. 'He wanted only rainbows for you, never the thunder clouds that racked Mees Daisy's life. Ah, she was so lovely, and she came to the *signore* too late from that husband of hers. Too late for him to set things right for her ... you understand? You are not a child any more. You are a young woman of twenty and you must accept the facts of life.'

'But, Crezia, he was only forty-five.' The bitter weeping shook Persepha again; the desolation of loss swept over her and made her feel as if she were drowning in loneliness ... that awful loneliness she had always feared. Marcus had always guarded her and kept her safe; been father-figure, mentor, and droll friend. His loss of Daisy had made him cynical in many respects, but Persepha had loved him beyond judgment or criticism.

'How shall I bear it?' she whispered to Lucrezia. 'What shall I do? Where shall I go?'

They both knew that Stonehill Mansion was entailed and must go to a nephew of Marcus's. The great stone house that had been her home for twenty years was no longer her home; this quaint old bedroom with its high fourposter bed was destined to pass into other hands, for the nephew was married and he had a family, and they were people who had never accepted her as a member of the Stonehill family.

'I – I feel like an outcast,' she said. 'I feel as if strong walls had collapsed around me and left me all alone and desolate. It's the worst feeling of my life, Crezia. It's almost more than I can bear.'

Yet somehow she did manage to endure the next few days and what happened during that time. Relations of her guardian came to Stonehill and made all the arrangements for the interment, which would be in the family vault, and it was Lucrezia who informed her that these people didn't wish her to attend the funeral. They wanted her to pack up and leave and would be giving her a cheque to tide her over until she found work of some sort.

It was incredible, not to be taken in that she was being treated like some creature with whom Marcus had lived who was now being bought off.

'To hell with the cheque,' she said, and tore it into fragments. Then she flung into a suitcase the less expensive garments bought for her by Marcus this season, and with tears of rage and grief in her hazel eyes she ran downstairs to the library and climbing on to a chair unhooked her mother's portrait from the wall, and was holding it, dust on her fingers, when the telephone rang in the silent hall.

She didn't wish to answer it, feeling too shaken, too upset by the way she had been thrust even out of Marcus's death, but it kept on ringing, insistently, and she finally went to the instrument and snatched it from the cradle.

'There's no one at home,' she said in a tear-thickened voice. 'The members of the family are attending a funeral.'

'That is you, Señorita Paget, who speaks?' The voice was deep, grating, and foreign, and instantly it conjured up for Persepha an image of a ruthless dark face from the realms of other worlds and pagan customs.

'This is she, *señor*. May I ask what you require?'

There was an instant of silence, and then the unusual voice struck again across her hearing. 'I require to see you, *señorita*, and I shall come for you in a car in a matter of minutes.'

'I shouldn't do that, *señor*,' she rejoined. 'I am leaving Stonehill – I have my marching orders and I shall be gone in a matter of minutes.'

'You will stay and wait for me,' he ordered. 'What I have to say to you concerns your guardian and a certain matter he and I discussed a few days before his demise. It is of the greatest importance that you remain to hear what I have to say – the Señor Stonehill would wish you to do this.'

'I – I can't imagine what you and Marcus would have discussed that concerned me,' she argued, for she was too torn by her personal conflict to care about seeing anyone, least of all the man from Mexico who struck her as being as pitiless as the Stonehill relations who were throwing her out of her home. 'I knew he gambled, but I had no part in all that—'

'I don't gamble, Miss Paget.' Now a whisper of the lash

came into the deep voice which would be accustomed to giving orders and having them promptly obeyed. 'What is it, are you afraid of seeing me again?'

Persepha stared at the panelled wall in front of the telephone table, and she felt the leaping of her nerves as the hall clock stirred and chimed. Friendly sounds at one time, announcing tea and buttered scones in the library with dear Marcus, but now the chimes were like small bells of doom, tolling the end of her life as well as her guardian's.

'I feel as if I shall never feel anything again,' she said to Don Diablo Ezreldo Ruy. 'Come if you must, *señor*. I shall be waiting out on the steps, for I no longer belong under the roof of Stonehill.'

And there she sat as the sleek car drew to a halt at the base of the stone steps, dark-clad and hatless, her suitcase beside her, with the portrait of her mother propped against the case. The car door opened and the long, lean figure emerged, clad impeccably in stone-grey. He came to the fourth step and stood looking at her, his unfathomable dark eyes fixed upon the pale blaze of her hair. Persepha gazed back at him, and it was obvious that she had been crying, for the marks of tears were on her cheeks, smudged with the dust from the back of the portrait which had never been moved from the day it had been hung.

'You have the dirty face of a child,' he said, and he took from his pocket an immaculate white handkerchief and tossed it into her lap. 'Wipe your eyes, *señorita,* and come with me.'

'I – I'll do no such thing—' She gave him a mutinous look. 'Who are you to give me orders?'

'The man,' he said deliberately, 'who is going to marry you.'

Persepha, who had already suffered a tremendous

shock, was so unprepared for his statement that she went almost as white as the handkerchief he had given her. Her fingers clenched the fine linen, and her eyes dwelt on his dark face with the expression of a bewildered, hurt child whom adults had suddenly decided to torment. Persepha, who for most of her life had been happy and secure with Marcus, now felt such an overwhelming sense of loss that the great tears welled again and ran down her lovely, dirty face.

'*Por deus—*' The Don suddenly bent over her, lifted her with that ease she remembered and carried her to his car, where he placed her on the back seat; where he left her while he fetched her suitcase, her mother's portrait, and the black straw hat she had bought in the village stores to wear with her only dark garment, a jersey wool dress with pearl buttons on it.

Don Diablo joined her in the car and deliberately closed the door. He took her in his arms and, this stranger with the devil's face, allowed her to weep all over the shoulder of his impeccable grey suit.

'We say in Mexico that there is a time for the wine and a time for the water; a time for tears and a time for cheers. Cry out your heart, *chica,* and then we shall talk together as man and woman.'

Man and woman, she thought vaguely. She and this man whom she barely knew, and yet who had talked of marriage? As she dried her eyes and mopped her face she saw the smudges of grime on what had been his snowy handkerchief, and it suddenly struck her that she must look a sight. In her dash from the bedroom which she would never sleep in again she had forgotten to comb her hair, and with her hair all over her messy face she must present a very unattractive picture.

The look that she gave the Don was a trifle defiant, for she had been reared by Marcus to be fastidious of her person and always well-groomed. Her world had truly turned awry for her to be looking like this!

'I'm afraid I've made a mess of your handkerchief, *señor*,' she said, and her voice that was always slightly husky had increased in huskiness. 'I'd offer to wash it, but I've been thrown out of Stonehill as if I'd never belonged there. My name should be Orphan Annie and there should be a storm . . . farcical, isn't it, that a girl of twenty should suddenly find herself homeless, moneyless, and not even trained to wash dishes! It should be good for a laugh, but I'm feeling too blue for laughing. I should be laying white roses on dear Marcus's coffin, but they said I wasn't a member of the family – they implied that I had no rights at all, though they allowed Lucrezia to attend because she was his nurse when he was a boy. Strange, but I never could imagine Marcus as a boy. He always seemed so adult and worldly.'

Persepha gazed directly into the face of the Spaniard, whose eyes were intent upon her face. 'I cared deeply for Marcus – there wasn't anything I wouldn't have done for him.'

'I am glad to hear that.' The dark eyes gazing back into hers were unreadable, and though deeply set they were not small eyes. Their lids were heavy, almost carved, and the length of his lashes intensified his secretive look. It seemed to Persepha that he had a dash of Indian blood in his veins, for his skin was bronzed rather than sallow, and his facial bones were firm and distinct beneath his skin, like those of the Aztec warriors of old Mexico. He might even be called noble-looking, and though there wasn't a thing about him that Persepha found physically unattractive, he aroused in her a certain fear that was physical.

She twined his handkerchief around her fingers and

glanced away from his eyes that seemed to penetrate into her very mind, there to read her thoughts with a disturbing clarity of vision and experience.

'Are you hungry, *señorita*? I imagine that you have not had a very satisfactory breakfast, and it is now close on lunch time.'

'I wasn't feeling hungry—' For some reason his concern startled her. 'But I suppose – yes, I could eat something right now.'

'Then let us eat,' he said, and lifted to the seat a lunchbasket which contained a cold roasted chicken, tomatoes, sticks of celery, sesame rolls and wine in a plaited straw bottle. There were also wine glasses on stems, and when the Don had poured the wine it gleamed tawny in the bowls.

'This you will have first of all.' He handed Persepha a glass of the wine and she saw from his face that he would brook no refusal. She accepted the glass, and her eyes dwelt gravely on his face as he murmured: '*Salud, señorita*. May the wine ease a little of your heartache.'

He was a strange man, she thought, and not to be denied, for she found herself drinking his wine and eating his food without demur. It was even enjoyable, as picnics usually are, and the wine had to be a fine one, and fairly potent, for soon the events of the last few days seemed to lose that sharp edge of pain and to become more bearable. At last, after the dessert of large sweet strawberries, Persepha let herself relax against the upholstery of the car seat, and her thoughts and feelings drifted awhile in the pain-killing haze induced by the wine, of which she had had two glasses.

It seemed for now that nothing very much mattered any more. Perhaps the arrogant Spaniard was going to seduce her, and there would be no guardian to take a whip to his shoulders, as Marcus had taken one to that reckless-eyed boy called Rashleigh, who had climbed the ivy to her bedroom, and had entered through the french windows to find her in nothing but her robe. It had been after midnight, after her nineteenth party had ended. Peter and his father Lord Rashleigh were staying as guests for the week-end, and it had been that young man's behaviour which had helped to make Persepha wary of men, even contemptuous of them. They seemed to want only one thing of a girl, and when she had cried out and Marcus had heard and thrashed Peter, she had watched and not cared that her guardian had used his whip and not his fists. She had always known that Marcus could be cruel when he liked, and offended by Peter, by the things he had said before Marcus had stormed into her room, she hadn't felt any pity for him.

'You said, Don Diablo, that you had something to say to me.' She heard the slight note of bravado in her voice, for it was a lonely feeling, a cut-loose and forlorn emotion, not to have Marcus around to defend her against men who wanted her just for her looks. She couldn't pretend not to know that she had a certain beauty, for she looked like Daisy, and each time she looked at Daisy's portrait she saw the fair and fragile attraction which had made a slave all his life of Marcus Stonehill. He had been the kind of man who could have had anyone he wanted, but he had chosen to be a bachelor all for the sake of a clergyman's daughter who had run off with an impecunious and unfaithful actor and gone on the stage which in the end had killed her. Marcus had made a goddess of Daisy, and in her own way Persepha had made a god of Marcus.

She looked at Don Diablo and saw a man with the face of a devil.

'Was your telephone call only an excuse to get me here?' she asked.

'I never make excuses, *señorita.*' He, too, lay back against the grey upholstery and his long fingers toyed with a flat gold cigarette-case. 'You permit that I smoke? I have noticed that you don't have the habit yourself.'

'Of course you may smoke, *señor.*' She said it almost eagerly, for every action that occupied his hands and his lips kept her free of what she was beginning to think would be an inevitable struggle. Though so tall, and so lean that he might have been a Toledo blade sheathed in fine cloth, there was a great look of strength about Don Diablo. It was there in his hands, his shoulders, and in that way he had of walking, as if in silent quest of prey.

'Marcus never liked me to smoke,' she added. 'He said it was bad for a woman's skin and caused wrinkles and a poor colour. He adored my mother, you see, and he always said that her skin was like rose petals that never faded. Roses were always his favourite flower, and that was why—' Persepha caught her breath. 'He could be cruel, you know, but he was never vindictive like those relations of his. They've treated me like his kept woman, but I was his ward. I know that some people thought otherwise because he was so good-looking, and a gambler, but Marcus loved me as if I were his daughter—'

'I know, *señorita.*' An unusual cigarette smoke drifted from the Don's aquiline nostrils. 'I come of a race who are swift at judging people, and you may rest assured that in the short while I knew Señor Stonehill, I very much respected him for a shrewd, quick-witted man, strangely honourable in his own fashion. Were you curious as to how we came to be acquainted?'

'Of course,' she said, breathing the smoke that seemed to hold a suggestion of an exotic, faraway place. 'I knew Marcus all my life and I travelled abroad with him, but we had never met you in any of those places, and he never mentioned a Don Diablo.'

'He and I never met before I came to Stonehill Mansion. It was a most curious mission that brought me, and a story he would have told you, had destiny not touched him on the shoulder and beckoned him away. You will listen patiently, *señorita*, while I tell it to you?'

'I seem to have nowhere else to go,' she said, with that little touch of humour which had always brought an answering glint to the grey eyes of Marcus. 'And I am rather fond of stories, *señor*.'

'This one is fact, not fiction, *señorita*,' he rejoined, and the carved eyelids narrowed across his eyes that were so dark as to be like jet. 'It is a tale that started in Mexico and ended, or very nearly, here in England. One day in my own country, on my own estate, I was riding a fresh young horse that shied from a snake and threw me to the ground, where I struck my head against a boulder and was knocked unconscious. In the fall my slouch hat became dislodged, and if I had lain in the full Mexican sunlight, senseless and hatless for even an hour, I should have woken with brain fever, or even a partial loss of my sight, for in high summer the sun is hot as in a desert land, fierce and penetrating, even for a skin as dark as mine. But as fortune would have it a covered wagon came by, the home on wheels of the travelling tinker, so tanned and ragged I thought him a Mexican until he spoke, in an amazingly cultured English voice. He covered me from the sun in the shade of the wagon, bathed my head with the precious water in his barrel, and in truth he saved my reason, if not my life.'

Don Diablo regarded the cigarette in his hand, in the ivory holder, and there was about his stern lips a faintly sardonic smile. 'We talked, that man and I, and I discovered that he had been for many years an actor on the English stage, not a very successful one, however, who when his young wife left him for another man, left England and became a seeker of his fortune in South America, Peru, and Argentine, until he had drifted into Mexico, there to work a little here, a little there, until he took to the life of an itinerant seller of pots, pans and patent medicines. I discovered that he amused me, for he had so many tales to tell, and my life at the hacienda was not a very sociable one. I invited this man to work for me in the capacity of an odd-job man, and he agreed, for he was not at that time in a good state of health and he welcomed the chance to have a more settled home. As I say, in many ways he was cultured, and we spent many evenings together, talking of the world and what we thought of it.'

The Don paused and regarded Persepha with thoughtful eyes. 'Yes, *señorita*, it was your mother whom you resembled, not your father. In that rugged, worn, tanned face his eyes were blue, and yours are a golden-brown.'

Persepha stared at the Don with those eyes of hers, which indeed had flecks of gold in them. What was he saying? What was he implying? That this man whom he had befriended in Mexico had been her *father*?

'Yes, Miss Paget.' The Don inclined his head as he read her eyes and saw the look of shock that flashed in them. 'When a final illness overtook Charles Paget he gave me a miniature which he always wore around his neck on a chain; it was of a beautiful woman, the girl who had been his wife, whom in his youth he had treated less than well. He admitted this, a matter of hours before he passed away. He knew that she had gone to the man who would have made her a far better husband, and because he knew that she was to have a child, and that Marcus Stonehill could take better care of her, he let the matter rest. But, before he died, he asked that if I ever came to England I would look up Stonehill and ensure that the child was happy and cared for, and this I did, Miss Paget, when a few weeks ago a matter of business brought me to this country.'

The Don removed the end of his cigarette from the holder and tossed it from the car window. He put the holder away in his pocket, and from that same pocket he took out the miniature on a chain about which he had spoken. Faded, worn by the sun of many countries, yet still discernible, the features that were so much like Persepha's, framed by the silvery-gold hair that dipped in a truant wave above the large eyes, pools of brown shimmering with a soft laughter.

'This lovely woman was your mother, *señorita*?'

'Yes,' Persepha whispered. 'And my father's name was Charles. But it's incredible, *señor*.' She held the miniature and visualized it around the sun-tanned neck of that travelling tinker who had walked out of her life all those years ago ... to walk back a ghost this strange, lost day when Marcus was laid to rest.

'Not incredible,' said the Don, 'but a stroke of fate. He left you to Marcus Stonehill, and now Marcus leaves you to me.'

Again the Don spoke words that seemed to strike to the centre of Persepha's heart, making it beat so fast that she felt she couldn't take a normal breath.

'What do you mean?' Her fingers clenched the miniature.

'Exactly what I say, *señorita*. I hold you – if this does not sound too melodramatic – in my power.'

'Only Marcus could say that,' she disputed hotly. 'Only he had power over me, and only because I wanted it that way.'

'You always did what he required of you, eh? You always abided by his wishes?'

'I loved him! He was the only person who cared two

halfpennies about me when my mother died. Of course I liked to please him by doing as he asked. It was my way of repaying him – for all my real father cared I could have gone into a home for foundlings!'

'I quite agree.' The Don leaned a little forward, fixing her with his eyes that had a mesmeric quality not quite human, or so it seemed to Persepha. Hawk's eyes, intent on his prey before he pounced. She drew back and away from him, pressing into the angle of her seat, and feeling real fear for the first time in her life.

'Your guardian,' he said deliberately, 'wished for you to become my wife. He and I discussed it one afternoon when I came to Stonehill, and because he knew of the precarious state of his health he desired to ensure that you would be secure for the rest of your life. Do you doubt me, *señorita*? You knew your guardian better than most. You must have known that he had it in mind to find a rich husband for you.'

Persepha crouched as tense as a young cat in a corner of the car, and though she wanted to cry out, to claw, to fight for her freedom, she was held immobile by the strange power of this man who came from another world and claimed her from the dear, dead hands of Marcus.

'You know that I speak the truth, don't you?' the Don's voice had softened, not with gentleness but with a sort of menace. 'You know that had he lived he would have told you himself that he approved my request to make you my wife.'

'But you don't know me – you don't love me,' she said hoarsely.

'In Mexico, *señorita*, the knowing and the loving come after the marriage.'

CHAPTER TWO

IT was a place out of a dream, but to Persepha it seemed more like a nightmare from which she couldn't awake.

She had married a man she hardly knew and the ceremony itself was a vague memory of the church of St. Anne, quite near to where she had lived with her guardian. There had been candles and roses, and a silver crucifix shining against the robes of the priest. There had been words spoken in Latin which she had not understood, and a pair of pure gold rings, one for her and one for Don Diablo. Then there had been a swift journey by car, and the coloured lights of the airfield glimmering through a sudden spate of rain ... but here in Mexico the sun shone as if reflected in the facets of a great diamond, and the high walls of the hacienda had a fabulous glow about them, which a gorgeous mantling of scarlet flowers turned into a vision, as if a splendid cloak had been tossed from the shoulders of a matador and flung across the stonework.

A place to love ... had she loved the Don her husband. But Persepha didn't even know him, and so the hacienda was like a prison set high on a rocky crag above a gorge that overflowed with huge blossoms, giant green ferns, and waterfalls that from high up looked like ribbons of liquid silver.

The Hacienda Ruy ... the Royal House as it was called by the several hundred people who lived and worked on the estate, which was so vast that Persepha didn't dare to wonder what the Don was worth in terms of land and cash and power. It was as if some feudal lord had come riding by and had snatched her for his own, and because it seemed as if Marcus had let his gambling soul be swayed by so much power and wealth, she had in a mood devoid of emotion let herself be married to a man who inspired her with a sort of fear rather than any desire of the heart, or the body her guardian had shielded from other men.

'Why the Royal House?' she had asked, and though she had meant to say it with scorn there had been something in her husband's look which had made her afraid to scorn him.

'I had an ancestress who was an Aztec priestess.' His smile had been a sardonic flicker on his lips chiselled like the rest of his face. 'The hacienda is built on the site of her temple. There in that gorge below us,' he had swept out a hand so the gold ring of alliance gleamed in the sun against his dark skin, 'a thousand of her people were slaughtered by the *conquistadores* from Spain. A Spanish nobleman forced the priestess to marry him, and a year to the day of the wedding she took her baby to the edge of the gorge and was going to leap off with him. But at the last moment she changed her mind about taking the helpless child with her to infinity and she left him to be found in the ferns by her husband. It was to her mind a Spanish child, and so she left him to found the family from whose roots I have sprung. So now you know, *queridisma*.'

Each time he used a Spanish term of endearment a shiver ran deep in Persepha. In England there had been a formality about him; in his way of dressing, in his attitude towards people.

But here in Mexico she began to glimpse a new side to him ... here he wore the close-fitting pants of the country, the white frilled shirt, and the black slouch hat pulled over a dark eye. He had, she suspected, a diverse personality and one that would be revealed to her as it suited him.

24

Already in her thoughts she was calling him Don Devil, and she gave a start almost of terror as in his silent way he came tall to her side of the high terrace balustrade, below which the gorge fell sheer in red and green, a place that drew her, fascinated her, especially so since the story he had told her.

'Our food is on the table, *mia*. It will grow cold and spoil, and the best cook in this region will be most annoyed with me.'

'Would that worry you, that a servant of yours should be annoyed?' Persepha turned from the cream stone of the terrace to look at him, and her gaze as always was defiant. 'I have the impression that not a thing on earth would ever truly ruffle your feelings.'

'You must then think me as hard as iron,' he said. 'Is that why you fear to come near me, in case your soft body should bruise and break against mine?'

His eyes seemed to glint, but she thought not with laughter, as they swept up and down her slim figure in the hyacinth-blue shirt and the pale-coloured, narrow-fitting trousers.

'In England I thought you lovely,' he said, in that voice that was extra meaningful because of its deep, foreign intonations. 'But here in my country you are even more unusual, for hair such as yours is like the white-gold which the cruel *conquistadores* made my people mine out of the depths of the earth.'

'Pluto's palace,' she said, with a quiet flippancy, her nerves made taut by his reference to her looks. 'You seem to forget that you have *conquistadore* blood in your veins as well, Don Diablo.'

'True,' he drawled, 'and it is likely to come to the surface if you continue to treat me as if I were a stranger instead of your husband. Now, *mi mujer*, we will go to the table and eat. The food you will find is Mexican, like my house, like my soul. Come!'

The noon light was brilliant with heat and only under the enormous lime tree was it partially cool, for it was where the lunch table had been laid, a beautiful lace cloth covering the circular, cane-plaited surface, with matching basket chairs in cane. On the table was an exotic arrangement of orchids, and wine in a basket, with glasses on those long stems that the Don was fond of toying with in his lean hands.

'Be seated.' He drew out her chair and she brushed against him as she sat down and was intensely aware of how tall he was, and how white was his shirt against the tawny skin of his body. Her beloved Marcus had been dark, but not nearly so dark as this man. He had been fairly tall, but he hadn't towered above her in this intimidating way. At times he had been stern, but he had never emanated this degree of physical and mental power.

'Fear takes the shape of a black panther in the night,' she had once read, and that curious unrealistic fear was hers right now. They were about to eat, but when she looked into his eyes a terror of the night rushed over her.

Since the conclusion of their wedding ceremony they had been travelling, and only now did it sweep over Persepha that she was 'home', if the hacienda could be called that, and today their life together really began.

'You will enjoy the food,' he said, 'once you accept that everything in Mexico has an extra dash of spice.'

Persepha shot him a look from beneath her lashes, for as always she suspected a double meaning in his words. White-coated Indians came to the table and began to pour the wine and to serve the food. All the time she could feel the Don silently watching her, there beneath the dappled shade of the lime-scented tree, faint shadows beneath her eyes, and her heart a rebellious weight in her breast.

Obeying Marcus even in his death she had married this man he had chosen for her ... in a blind daze of grief and hopelessness she had been led to an altar which now felt like a sacrificial stone.

'We will drink a toast.' Don Diablo lifted his wine glass, in which the wine was as glintingly red as the rubies on Persepha's left hand. 'Come, join me, *mia*, for in truth this is our wedding breakfast.'

'You realize—' Her teeth caught at her lip. 'You must know that I've made a terrible mistake in marrying you. I – I was out of my mind over Marcus, and now—'

'Now it's too late for regrets,' he broke in, his voice as deceptively smooth as silk. 'You are my wife, I am your husband.'

'But only in words!' She leaned forward, an eager pleading in her eyes. 'A marriage such as ours can be annulled, for we haven't – we aren't totally bound.'

'But soon we shall be.' There was a whisper of ice in his voice, the kind that covers the cone of a volcano. 'I request that you lift your glass so that we might pledge each other, for I have no intention of letting you go, *querida*. You married me in a Catholic church, and on each hand you wear my rings; the golden ring of alliance, and the Ezreldo Ruy rubies which in their time have had real blood on them.'

'Are you threatening me?' she whispered, and her own blood felt as if it ran cold as she looked into his adamantine eyes, dark as the night that fell upon Mexico when the sun died away.

'I should be honour bound to execute punishment if you should try and run away from me, but let me warn you that you won't get very far. The boundary lines of my land are limitless and on that land live only my people.

27

We are not in England any more, *chica*. Here in all truth I am the master of all I survey, and if what lies a thousand miles away is mine, then think how much is mine that my eyes look upon across the mere width of a table.'

'You are quite ruthless, aren't you?' Persepha had never been more sure of anything as she looked across at those features that were as if hammered from bronze, the black hair sweeping back from the broad forehead that betokened a powerful brain. It was that brain allied to the Spanish ruthlessness which had helped to make him the master of so much territory. Her master, from whom at present there seemed no escape.

Persepha lowered her gaze and picked up her wine glass, obeying the female instinct that told her that only by discovering the weak rents in his armour would she be in a better position to fight with him. Right now she hardly knew him. She was like one of those brides whose marriage had been arranged to a man unknown to her.

'What toast have you in mind?' she asked, bittersweetly. 'A reassertion that I honour and obey you?'

'I know very well, Persepha, that I can make you honour and obey me.'

'Oh, then I hope that you didn't have it in mind to ask a pledge of love from me.' She thrust up her chin and dared a direct meeting with his unnerving eyes. His was the gaze of the basilisk, scattering into atoms the will of another person. 'Whatever you get from me, it will never be love, Don Diablo.'

'Brave words, *querida*.' His gaze grew mocking as he raised his glass until a shaft of sunlight caught it and the facets and the red wine glowed in unison. 'May you always be as courageous as you are right now, always as fair, and always as furious. It has never been my nature to want a dove in my nest, so today as the sun shines there come together a dark eagle and a white mate. To you, *esposa mia, te quiero!*'

Her heart thumped. 'I want you!' he had said in Spanish. Had she hoped that he might say, 'I love you!' so that she might have a whip-hold over him?

'To you, *esposo mio*.' Defiantly she raised her glass. 'May I die before I ever want you!'

'Gracias!' His sardonic expression was unaltered by her words, and after setting down his wine glass he proceeded to eat his food. 'This is excellent, *querida*. You really must eat and get some colour back into your cheeks, for when they have that wild-rose flush you are truly the loveliest creature on earth.'

'I wish to heaven I was ugly,' she flung at him. 'You wouldn't want me then. You'd be repelled, for it's obvious from what I've seen so far of your surroundings that you like everything to please your proud eyes.'

'Tell me, my bride, do you really think that your most excellent Marcus would have wanted you had you been an ugly child instead of one who resembled the woman he adored? He saw in you a miniature of her; had it been otherwise I venture to say that he would have placed you in an orphanage and forgotten about you.'

'That's a cruel, unjustified thing to say!' Persepha looked at her husband with eyes that hated him. 'Marcus had a heart! He wasn't like you – Lucifer; you want heaven and hell combined, so that you can be godlike and satanic at one and the same time.'

'And hell hath no fury like the bride of Satan, eh?' Abruptly he smiled and his teeth were incredibly white against his skin, and perfect as an animal's teeth might be. 'The food, at least, is heavenly, and so are many parts of my house. Later on I will escort you on a tour of inspection and you may judge for yourself, for even if you can't admire me, you may find it in your heart to admire the hacienda. It was erected a hundred years ago and has been embellished ever since, and don't tell me that you don't like things that please your own proud eyes, my dear.'

'I expect I shall admire the place,' she said, eating her small potatoes that were baked with the meat and served with ears of sweet corn. The meat was tender and succulent, and the sauce had a delicious spicy taste that added to the pleasure of eating. That Persepha was hungry she couldn't deny, for she had not eaten properly for several days. She had been too dazed, too stricken, but now she was coming fully awake to her situation and her surroundings, and only by letting her youth find its strength again would she be able to combat the magnetism of this man.

She gazed past that arrogant, haughty profile into the Moorish patio that could be glimpsed beyond a chiselled archway, the twin columns of which were a twining mass of brilliant mauve flowers. Set back from the archway and framed like a picture was a fountain of pure green marble, ornament of classic perfection, with miniature waterfalls tumbling from bowl to bowl, the magic of the water and the sun forming a rainbow that never faded.

That she saw beauty whichever way she turned was undeniable ... but when she looked at Don Diablo she saw a formidable foe instead of a fond companion, as Marcus had so often been. Her throat muscles tightened, her eyes ached, and she was afraid she might cry again. She blinked rapidly and took a sip of wine.

'Does the sun try your eyes?' The Don looked at her narrowly. 'It will seem fierce for a while, for in England you never see sunlight so dazzling, eh? It is moderate like the emotions of the people there. Polite and shy of flaunting itself as it does in Mexico. When you walk in our sun you must always remember to wear a hat ... I will find

30

you a Mexican straw so that the wide brim will shield your fair skin.'

'Are you afraid I shall go red as a beet and peel like a dried onion?' she asked flippantly. 'If that is the case, then I shall do my best to get sunburned.'

'Neither sunburn nor sunstroke will be pleasant for you, so stop talking like a child.' The look he gave her was menacing, with not a hint of humour in it. 'If at any time you dare to go bareheaded, then I promise that you will learn a lesson from me that you won't forget in a hurry. I don't imagine that you have ever been spanked, but if you foolishly defy me in the matter of headgear when you go walking or riding, then I shall turn you over my knee and mark that white skin of yours with the flat of my hand. I mean what I say, Persepha. Behave childishly and I shall treat you as if you are a child.'

'Can I take that as a firm promise?' she asked, and gave a defiant toss of her head as a manservant came to the table and murmured some words to the Don in the local dialect which she didn't understand, though she knew a smattering of Spanish from a holiday she had taken with Marcus in the south of Spain. She still remembered that cruel bullfight, and as Don Diablo rose from the table and excused himself for a few minutes, she saw that he had the lean hard grace of body, and the ruthless looks of the matadors of Spain. She could imagine him with a sword in his hand, his eyes fixing the bull as he plunged the blade to the very heart of the beast. Persepha was certain that he would have no fear, no hesitation, no regret as the blood spilled on to the sand.

He walked away from the table with his long silent stride, and just a few moments later the servant brought dessert to the table, a delectable concoction of sliced pineapple and papaya with tiny quarters of orange and a jug of rich cream.

31

Persepha ate her sweet in a suspended mood of peace which she ardently wished could last without interruption from the disturbing personality of the man she had married in haste.

She could hear the soft splashing of the fountain of green marble, and the trilling of bright-winged birds in the many colourful trees that surrounded the courtyards and smaller patios. Finches and tanagers, she thought idly, for this place would invite both tame and wild birds to its exotic blossoms and its lush leafy plants. Her gaze followed the mocking-birds and the flame-tailed humming-birds that flew in and out of the tangled creepers like whirling toys gaily painted.

She was half a world away from England, and this was the place she must now accept as home, for she no longer had a home in her own land. Strangers now resided at Stonehill, which, towered and grey-stoned, had no resemblance to the Hacienda Ruy. In fact, if Marcus had not been master there it would have been rather a grim house, yet even so Persepha had never thought of it as she did this Spanish dwelling ... as a prison that held torment for her, unless she found some means of escaping from the place.

Then, even in the midst of her thoughts, she felt the approach of her husband and she tensed in her chair and the look of introspection fled from her eyes to be replaced by the wary look of a creature snatched away from familiar surroundings into realms where a devil walked among the roses.

Her eyes flicked the Don's face as he sat down; his features were grim and the chiselled lips were drawn into hard, thin lines. He sat there silently while the manservant brought coffee to him in a shining silver pot. Persepha felt the beating of her heart ... she knew instinctively that he had been giving someone a bit of hell, and she caught her breath when he looked directly at her as if reading her mind.

'Yes,' he said curtly, 'I have just had the unwelcome duty of kicking someone off this estate. He was a groom who has so mishandled one of my horses that its mouth is damaged, and when I left you just now it was because I had been told that the horse had backed this man into a corner of his stall, where he might have kicked him to death. A misused horse can turn as dangerous as a tiger.'

'Oh?' she said, totally uncaring that the horse could have mauled him in its state of pain and anger. 'Is that why they use the poor brutes in Spain to be gored by bulls? Because having been hurt and mishandled they turn dangerous and make better sport for your blood-thirsty people?'

The Don heard her out and just looked at her, calmly lifting his cup and drinking the dark aromatic coffee to which he had not not added cream or sugar.

It must be bitter as gall, she thought, pouring about half an inch of the thick cream into her own cup. It was as she lifted her cup and took a sip of her own coffee that she caught sight of the long rent in the shoulder of her husband's white shirt, and when she saw the dark skin gleaming through she realized that he had had the task of getting the infuriated horse away from the stablehand who had hurt him.

'You have seen a bullfight?' Don Diablo asked her, his eyes intent upon her face as he tossed a quarter of orange into his mouth.

'Yes, and I hated it,' she replied tensely. 'I was repelled by the delight of the crowd in so much torture and pain. No wonder the *conquistadores* were so abominably cruel when they came from a country like Spain. Slaughtering poor defenceless Indians must have been quite a sport for them.'

'The Indians were never all that defenceless, for they had a few refined methods of torture of their own.' A smile flickered on the lips that were as well cut as those on a golden Inca mask. 'One of their most popular methods was to make a captive Spaniard swallow boiling oil or even gold. Believe me, *querida*, there is a deep-lying streak of cruelty in men of most countries, even your own.'

'I doubt if any Englishman has ever gone to the extremes of cruelty that your Latin races have. Why, you said yourself that we English were more moderate.'

'In your loving was what I meant,' he drawled, leaning back in his basket chair and taking from his hip pocket not a flat gold case this time but a well-handled leather one from which he selected a slim cigar of such a darkness of leaf that it looked absolutely lethal when he placed it between his white teeth. He struck a match, applied the flame, and emitted a strong smoke from his nostrils.

'Tell me, *chica*,' that sardonic note was in his voice, 'has it not drifted across your mind once or twice that your guardian was rather cruel in giving you into my hands? It surely bewilders you that he must have put mercenary values before emotional ones, and cared more that you have a rich husband than a fond one. Did you not tell me when you placed your hand in mine that you married me for his sake; because it was his last wish here on earth?'

'Yes,' her voice was husky, 'I did what he wanted, but I do ask myself why. I do wonder if he ever regretted loving Daisy so much that it closed his heart against any other woman. I do wonder if he felt that love was too shattering an experience, and that it would be better if I never felt it, never knew it, never had to endure finding

34

and losing it. That would be like Marcus ... but it wouldn't be like him to be cruel ... to me.'

'Perhaps not.' The Don shrugged his shoulders and lifted his dark gaze to the lime tree, through whose leaves and branches the sky gleamed a dazzling blue. 'He wished to know about Mexico and I described to him this land I have known all my life, and loved, though you seem to doubt that it is in me to feel such an emotion.'

'Oh,' she said, and she could put a lot of expression into that small word, 'I don't doubt your ability to love what you own. This hacienda, your horses, your miles and miles of fertile land. You are a feudal throwback, Don Diablo. You spring from the loins of ruthless and predatory men and you have to take what you want, regardless of the feelings of the women who cross your path.'

'So it's land I love, bricks and mortar, and mettlesome horses.' He tipped cheroot ash with a quizzical expression. 'So you don't credit me with the ability to love one woman until my dying day, as your guardian did.'

'Quite frankly, no,' she said, and blew softly on a ladybird which had settled on the palm of her hand. The minute wings fluttered and the tiny thing flew away, and Persepha gave a sigh. If only she had wings and could just lift off into the air like Psyche. Instead she was like her namesake, who while playing in the fields of youth had been carried off by the lord of darkness, to his kingdom of Hades.

'What has happened to your stablehand?' she asked. 'Did you thrash him? Yes, I can see from your face that you did. Oh well, Marcus once thrashed a young man for trying to seduce me, so you have that much in common with him.'

'Tell me about this young man.' The dark eyes grew piercing. 'You were fond of him? You encouraged him to think that he could make love to you?'

35

'No! and don't go all inquisitorial, just like the traditional Latin husband.' She gave a laugh, but it wasn't a very humorous one. 'If you thought I wasn't virtuous would you throw me out? I have heard that Spaniards place inordinate value on the innocence of their brides, and it would be a laugh on you if I were shopsoiled instead of brand new.' All at once the idea was tempting that she lay claim to a lack of innocence that she knew would appal him. His high pride would never suffer a bride who was not virginal ... in all things he had to be first; the conqueror who plundered and took.

'If you had ever known a man, then I would know.' The Don spoke with that absolute assurance which she found so infuriating.

'Are you never wrong, about anything?' she asked stormily. 'Do you think you're the only man who has ever wanted this face all smiles for him, this body all weak with desire? When I was fifteen Marcus told me all about men and what it was they wanted if they thought a girl was pretty. He said they didn't want intelligence from an attractive girl, they wanted compliance and a weak will. Each holiday from my boarding-school we travelled in Europe and he taught me to like good paintings and works of art; music and the architecture of lovely old buildings. He gave me a mind to think with, and so every time a young man started lying his head off about loving me, I knew that all he really wanted was to paw me and make me feel cheap.'

Persepha smiled, bitter-sweetly. 'No, you have a bargain, Don Diablo, if all you want is a pristine body. What heart I had is buried with Marcus. What love I had to give, I gave to him. You, Señor Conquistadore, have but the shape of me, a thing of marble with hardly any feelings at all. Impeccable, cold, and heartless. A statue if you like, but not a woman.'

'So you think it beyond my powers to make you feel like a woman?' His eyes glinted and a certain *diablerie* seemed to drift into them, so that the eyelids drooped and the black lashes cast shadows on the chiselled bronze of his face. 'You are twenty and totally inexperienced, and I have been a man since before you were born. You make a challenge, *chica*, and I am too much a Latin not to accept it. *En verdad*, we will see whether or not I can bring alive a pale marble statue.'

'And if you don't?' she challenged, Will you let me go?'

'I never let go, *querida*, of what is mine.' And as if to set the seal on his words he ground out the stub of his cheroot with a decisive movement of his hand, and in a shaft of sunlight his gold ring glittered like his eyes.

'Then I hope,' Persepha said deliberately, 'that I catch some foreign germ and die before I have to spend the rest of my life with you!'

A lingering silence followed her words, which she had flung at him across the table with all the despair of a girl who in a matter of days had lost all that she had lived for. Words that she meant with all the heart that she denied.

Then, making every nerve in her body cry out with protest, the Don brought his hand down hard on the table and the things of porcelain and silver shook as if thunder cracked. 'You will not speak in such a way, do you hear me? This land is Mexican and here the old gods lurk in the shadows and listen to what we say, and I have an old *vecina* in my house, Carmenteira, who will tell you that the gods grant more readily our sinful wishes than our saintly ones. You little fool! One would think that you had married the Devil himself!'

'I have,' she rejoined, and it seemed to her that his dark, black-browed, fearsomely boned face could only

37

belong to that satanic deity. 'I see no angel when I look at you – only the dark angel!'

And this time, it seemed, she had gone beyond his tolerance of what he would take from a bride, and what he would punish. In an instant he was on his feet and striding round the table. He reached with long arms for her inwardly quaking figure and swung her with cruel strength out of her chair and up against his hard, powerful body. The warmth of his skin struck through the silk of her shirt, and his fingers bit into her flesh. She shuddered with pain and fright, and like a wild thing she began to struggle, even going so far as to kick at him with her sandalled feet. But as if he felt nothing but anger he dragged her closer to him and doubling his fist in her fine hair jerked back her head and made her cry out again. He bent to her and even as she fought with him, he took her lips with a fierceness that brooked no refusal. The strength in his arms could have cracked her body as he forced her to yield to his kiss, the entire length of her slim body pressed to his in the sort of embrace she had always before eluded with a lighthearted laugh, aware that if a man pursued her, there was always Marcus to protect her.

Now she had no protection from the frightening male strength of this man, who was no hopeful, ardent boy, but the man who had every right to hold her so, and kiss her until she felt her breath would stop.

When her feet left the ground and she realized that he was carrying her towards the hacienda, an incredible fury shook her and like a young vixen she sank her teeth into his shoulder and saw through the veil of her hair the drops of blood against the white material. Oh God, she had bitten him like some animal! At once she was torn between the delight of having hurt him, and fear of his retaliation.

'What are you doing?' She struggled in vain for her release from his arms whose muscles were like cords around her. 'Where are you going?'

He looked swiftly down in her eyes as he mounted a flight of iron-wrought stairs, taking them two at a time, and there was a look in his eyes that made Persepha want to scream. Never in her life before had she seen a look such as the one that burned in the Don's eyes, while across his hot forehead lay a thick strand of black hair.

'Aren't you woman enough to know?' he taunted her, and beside his mouth a pulse was beating, holding her mesmerized as he strode along the gallery, making for the bedroom which she had occupied last night ... on her own. Though she had known that it adjoined his room, he had not come near her, or touched her ...

Now was different and she knew it with her every nerve and instinct. The door of her room was thrust open and she was carried across to the great bed with its silk sheets and heavy lace coverlet. She was dropped without ceremony on to the lace and silk, and then he returned to the door and very deliberately turned the key in the lock.

Persepha pushed the hair from her eyes and watched him with terrified comprehension, with limbs that just wouldn't move as he came back to her, tall and powerful in the beautiful bedroom hung with flounced curtains and a huge vicuna rug spread over the floor.

The Latin eyes seemed to smoulder with points of fire in that dark, strong face, and she watched numbly as he unbuttoned his shirt and wrenched it with a single movement from his broad shoulders. She saw the marks of her teeth against the tawny skin, and the way the black pants fitted close to his lean hips and long legs.

He stood there studying her, and he looked every inch a man without mercy, in whom a rage of passion was building up ... and then he reached for her and his touch brought her alive ... desperately alive, so that she fought with a frightened fury that actually made him smile, his teeth glinting white and devilish as he pinned her to the bed with his hard body.

'Come, *mi mujer*,' he mocked. 'This is no way for a bride to treat her bridegroom.'

'Go – go to the devil!' she panted, swiftly turning her head aside so that his lips crushed the side of her neck. Her senses swam and for just a moment she seemed to see again that little church in the English hills, where the smoke of candles had mingled with the scent of roses. If she had thought not to awake from the dream, or the nightmare, then her hope was shattered. Marriage wasn't just words and a pair of rings on a prayer book ... it was this, a man with a woman ...

'*Viva mia*, I thought I was the devil,' and with a strength that mocked her, he turned her to him, and she closed her eyes as his lips breathed 'devil' against her lips.

CHAPTER THREE

It was several hours later when Persepha stirred awake to find her bedroom in velvety darkness.

She lay quiet under the silk sheets, and as awareness seeped back into her body and her mind, the quietness became torment, and with a sudden sob she turned and buried her face in the silk pillow.

The silk was smoky, tangy, and she tensed as suddenly as if a whip had stolen across her skin. The masculine aroma brought memory, and a wave of sweeping hot colour that seemed to envelop her from head to heels, and then it slowly receded and she felt shivery, forlorn, with an ache in her heart as well as her limbs.

Nothing had moved him, not pleas or raking finger-nails. With a strength whose recollection was enough to awake fear in her heart, he had made the spoken vows a living reality. He had wiped out the world she had always known and made a woman of the girl whom Marcus had always guarded so well. There had been no shield, no armour against Don Diablo, and as she lay clenching the sheet that covered her, her fingertips still seemed to feel the smooth warm skin of a masculine back that had rippled with firm muscle ... even a kind of beauty ... a terrible beauty she just didn't want to remember.

She closed her eyes and wished fiercely that she could kill him ... if there had been a knife handy she would have plunged it into him, and wouldn't now be a shivering, hot-cold piece of womanhood, far from all she had cared for and with no one ... not a soul to whom she could turn for sympathy in her plight.

Oh God, she hated self-pity, and sitting up she

41

wrapped her slim arms about her updrawn knees and stared into the duskiness that had given way to all that hot sunlight ... she had married him, knowing from the start that he meant to be a husband, not a guardian. She had stood in church with him and heard him speak of worship and obedience ... again she shivered, and then gritted her teeth like a young animal in distress. 'I hate you!' She spoke into the darkness, fiercely. 'I hate your black eyes and your black heart!'

Then because the darkness of her room made the details of her bridal all that more vivid, she leaned over to where a lamp stood on a night table and switched on the light. She stared at the pillow beside her, at the impression left by his dark head ... it was unbearable to remember that he had lain there, holding her.

Oh God, she just had to think of something else, and she let her gaze travel around the room and directed her hate at the unique beauty of it all. The lower half of the walls panelled in a dark wood that gleamed like silk, a sort of jungle wood, no doubt, that couldn't be attacked by termites. The upper half of the walls had a golden tinge to them, a most attractive foil for the beautifully carved wardrobe and vanity table, and the cascades of flounced netting at the long windows, also tied back from the high carved bed. The huge vicuna rug was thick and curly, and in front of the vanity mirror stood an array of crystal containers, round-bodied, long-necked, silver-topped, with a little carved golden box to one side, and a brush and comb set in gleaming ivory.

A sensuous room, deliberately designed for a woman, to set off those feminine attractions that would arouse a man each time he stepped from his own formal room into this soft, scented boudoir ... this gilded cage ... this passionate prison.

Her nostrils quivered at the subtle scent, in which

mingled that tang of a strong cheroot and the hard, clean sweat of a male body still clinging to the silk sheet which Persepha held around her. There on the rug lay her torn shirt, her trousers with the legs pulled inside out, her scraps of lingerie. One half of her wanted to rise and dress, but the other half was indolent, still faintly drowsy, still in a state of shocked sensibilities that shrank from contact with another human being. The very thought of having to face Don Diablo ever again was enough to bring a look of terror into her eyes.

No! Oh no, she couldn't bear it! She'd die if she had to see him ... that predator ... that inhuman devil who called himself her husband.

That was what he had whispered, his fist doubled in her hair. 'Now I'm your husband, *querida*. Now you are my wife.'

Even as she was shuddering, and trying to reject with her mind and her body that which could not be rejected, the door of her room suddenly opened. Persepha tensed, and then relaxed just a fraction as the old servant Carmenteira came into the room. She carried a small tray on which stood a tall slim glass of something that looked cool and inviting.

'I bring a little refreshment for the *señora*,' she said, and as she came to the side of the bed her black, deep-set eyes were flickering over Persepha, and in their depths was a wickedly amused awareness of what had taken place in this bedroom. She glanced from the girl crouching in a silk sheet to the garments on the floor, and a sly cackle broke from the old woman.

'So the proud little mistress has been taught her first lesson, eh?' Carmenteira held out the tray to Persepha. 'Passion-fruit juice, *señora*. Sweet and cool at the same time, as men sometimes like their women.'

Persepha took the glass of juice because she was feeling

43

abominably dry, but she wasn't going to take insolence from this old creature, just because she had lived in this house for years and was no doubt feared as a bit of an old witch.

'Thank you for bringing me a drink,' she said coldly. 'I shan't want anything more, so you can go now.'

'I have come to wait on the *señora*. To ensure that she is all right, then I will go.' Carmenteira bent to pick up the ripped blue shirt and the tangled trousers. 'A pity about the upper garment, which is the colour of flowers, but a woman was not meant to wear the trousers, not in the house of a real man. You have learned, have you not, that Don Diablo is every inch a real man, and that with him a woman is a woman or she is nothing?' Again that knowing cackle, that glance of mockery from eyes which had seen many things in their many years. She came close to the bedside and reached out a wrinkled hand to Persepha's bare arm. There against the soft white skin lay the mark of a dark bruise, and the old woman touched the bruise, almost as if it were a medal that Persepha had been given.

'I wondered why he should want a white young thing like you, but now I see the reason.'

'Do you?' Persepha ran her tongue round her lips, moist and sweetened now by the passion juice. 'To hurt and torment me, I suppose, for he certainly doesn't love me.'

'Love?' Old Carmenteira looked scornful. 'What is love? One can feel that for a kitten, a plant, a book! Between a man and woman it has to be passion ... a battle ... a winning and a losing. You were a virgin, that is a certainty if *he* married you. The fruit juice is good, eh? It makes you feel refreshed, for after a woman has been loved, she is always eager for three things. A glass of something cool, the feel of water on her skin, and a veil behind which to hide for a while. I am right, am I not, *señora?* I am not so ancient that I forget all about youth and its fires – the way they smoulder and leap and have to be quenched.'

'I – I don't want to talk about it, if you don't mind.' Persepha placed the empty glass on the tray, and there was a flush of mortification in her cheeks. If this old creature knew what had taken place, then so did the entire household. Fury rose up in Persepha and she just had to give way to it.

'What are you waiting about for?' she demanded. 'Do the Don's people want to hang the bed sheet on the hacienda gate so that everyone will be assured that he has bought himself a proper sort of bride?'

At this outburst Carmenteira stared at Persepha, then her expression altered slightly and a faintly sympathetic look came into her eyes in their deep bed of wrinkles.

'The English don't like to speak of these things, eh? You are shy of an old woman like me coming into the privacy of your bedroom – be easy, *señora*, and don't agitate yourself. Don Diablo sent me to you, for don't you know that I was the personal servant of his lady mother? I cared for her, the dark Madonna, until the day she died. Now I shall take care of his golden Madonna—'

'No – I can take care of myself and don't need your assistance.' Persepha dragged the silk sheet closer around her. 'Go and tell him! Tell him I don't want him, or you, or anyone else in this God-forsaken house. Tell him I hate him and everything he stands for – pride, arrogance, cruelty. You name it, he personifies it! I – I'd like to see him cold on the ground with his eyes out!'

This time Carmenteira backed away from the bed and swiftly crossed herself. She gazed at Persepha with a sort of horror in her eyes. 'A wife should not talk like that,' she

45

reproved. 'The evil one might hear you—'

'As far as I'm concerned the Don is the devil himself – and now get out and leave me alone! For heaven's sake go to your witch brews and your valedictions and put a curse on me. I'd like to get out of *his* clutches, one way or the other.'

'It isn't right the way that you speak, *señora*,' the old woman repeated. 'There are women all over Mexico who would be proud and eager to be the bride of Don Diablo, who is considered *el magnifico* of all this region, with much land, much power, and the ability to give pleasure to a dozen women, let alone one. You should feel honoured—'

'Honoured?' Persepha gave a scornful laugh. 'I feel insulted and degraded, for he doesn't even pretend to have a spark of affection for me. I merely arouse the animal in him – is that what Mexican women feel proud of, being mere objects of their master's—' Persepha broke off, for she couldn't endure to think of the word, let alone to say it. To be used and not loved was hell itself, and she flung away from old Carmenteira, hiding herself in her own loosened hair, which was long because Marcus had liked it that way.

Marcus! Oh – hell, if Marcus could see her now would he be so proud of having found her a rich husband? Oh God, had he been so blinded by the Don's wealth that he hadn't seen what sort of a man he was? Arrogant, self-willed, concerned only to please himself and his lean, wickedly graceful body?

It was as if a flame of hellfire itself licked through Persepha as she remembered the feel of that hard body, brown and warm as a saddle in the sun, with arms of steel that had wrapped themselves around her so there was no escape ... no avoidance of the lips that crushed her cries to tiny moans.

'Go away,' she said again. 'Leave me alone.'

'You will not be foolish, *señora*?'

'Foolish?' Persepha smiled wearily. 'Could I ever be more of a fool than I have been already? I married the Devil, didn't I?'

'There is a balcony out there beyond those windows, and women of this household have been foolish in various ways. The tiles of a courtyard are harder on a woman's body than even a loveless bed, and it would be a pity to break your white body, for in all truth the Don has only bruised it a little.'

Persepha could feel those bruises, a distant ache not nearly so acute as the ache she felt in her heart.

'Don't worry,' she said. 'I'll see him dead first.'

'Then I will go,' said Carmenteira, as if old woman that she was she had grown weary of trying to placate a girl not of her own people. 'Will it please the *señora* a little better if I send one of the maids to assist in the bathroom and to lay out a dress for the evening?'

'I shall be all right.' Persepha shuddered at the prospect of the evening ahead of her. 'I'm used to looking after myself and don't require to be waited on like a helpless ninny. Tell your master that I – that I would prefer to remain up here in my room.'

'Very well, *señora*. I will tell him that, but not the other – that you would like to see him with his eyes out. That would be too unkind, I think.'

'Does he deserve kindness?' Persepha muttered. 'I think not!'

A moment later she heard the door close behind the old woman, and she breathed a sigh of relief. Thank heaven to be alone again, and gathering the sheet around her bare body she made for the alcove door that led into the bathroom. The bath was huge and set round with steps of

47

pale green marble, with taps of solid silver. Persepha mounted the steps, letting the sheet fall away from her. As she turned on the hot water tap she saw herself reflected in the mirror that completely filled the wall at the side of the bath.

As the steam rose like a gauzy veiling, Persepha stared at herself in the mirror. Outwardly she looked no different, apart from the marks of his handling and the disarray of her pale shining hair. Her eyes were shadowed, but it was on the inside that she was altered. Quite ruthlessly the girlhood had been kissed out of her, and as she placed her hands against her body she realized, with a frightening thump of her heart, that she could have a baby.

The Don's baby ... child of Satan ... born of terror instead of love.

Persepha stepped quickly into her bath and sank down into the scented water. She snatched a container filled with soft green soap and emptied half the contents into the water; it quickly foamed and soon she was sitting in a white froth of soap bubbles, scrubbing fiercely at her skin with a loofah.

If only she could scrub away his touch as she scrubbed away his scent. If only she could step from this bath a girl again ... but she never could. The old days were gone for good, and no more would she hear the sound of men playing cards in the library at Stonehill, laughing loudly, looking at her with admiration, but from whom she was kept safe by Marcus.

It was ironical that he had kept her safe from comparatively harmless men, only to hand her over before he died to a man like Don Diablo. It had been unforgivable of him, and yet because of the love in her heart she could forgive him.

It was her husband whom she could never forgive.

48

When she had finished bathing she found a towelling robe behind the door and put it on. It came long on her and she knew instantly that it was the kind of robe worn by men; she would have flung it off again had there been anything else at hand. With tightened lips she looked in the mirror at herself and rolled up the sleeves. His robe, after all, was less intimate than the touch of his skin had been, and instantly her own skin was tingling and flushed, and her knees felt weak as she went back into her bedroom.

How long would it take to forget? – and then as her gaze fell upon the disordered bed she knew that there would be no merciful end to the memory. She had looked into his eyes and she had seen the way they had smouldered. He had taken her and would take her again ... to satisfy his arrogance and to please his pride.

How could she ever forget the supple, languid way he had stretched beside her, like a tiger pleased, holding her hand in that pelt of hair across his chest, pressing her fingers to the medallion that was the same golden tone as his skin. Dark warm gold, overlaid by dark hair.

Persepha flung up her hands and covered her eyes, but the memory and the vision wouldn't go away.

She went to her wardrobe, gazing without interest at the clothes it contained. Before they had left England, the day before their wedding, the Don had taken her to a big shop in London and there she had been equipped with a trousseau of exquisite dresses and outfits; coats, and shoes, and accessories. There they were arranged on the padded hanger and in colourful array on the cedarwood shelves, but they excited no admiration in Persepha; no desire to wear what the Don had bought her.

She needn't dress up, for she had decided to remain in her room and would eat up here whatever the man-servant brought to her. Her hand reached for one of the simple dresses she had brought from Stonehill and was half-way into it, reaching behind her for the zip, when her bedroom door swept open without ceremony. She heard the slight creak of the door and thought that Carmenteira had returned, or sent one of the maids to assist her.

'You may help me with this zip if you like,' she threw over her shoulder.

But the hand that took hold of her and held the zip in abeyance was not feminine. The voice that spoke struck through Persepha like a shaft. 'For our first evening together at the Hacienda Ruy you will wear something a little more fetching, *querida*. Something I gave you, which has no memories of any other man attached to it.'

She stood utterly still in his grasp, feeling again those hands that had not spared her when she had pleaded with him. That she had pleaded with him and lost her pride was more unbearable than anything had been, and this time she endured his touch and made of her face a cool mask.

'I wish to remain here in my room,' she said. 'I told the old woman to tell you—'

'Yes, so you did, but what I am told and what I desire are two separate issues.' He swung her to face him and though she shrank inwardly all through her body she retained that cold look of dignity with which she had decided to oppose him. She had learned that he liked to fight for her, and there was nothing, not a thing on earth, she would ever do willingly for him.

She looked at him and it felt like the bravest thing she had ever done to meet those eyes which knew her as no other man had ever known her; to see again their intense darkness which had smouldered with a passion which had seemed unholy. She tensed at the white splendour of his dinner jacket, and saw in the white frills of his shirt-front the gleam of jade buttons that matched his cuff-links. He was dressed as if for a wedding celebration, and she supposed coldly that for him there was something to celebrate.

'I'm not in the mood for an elaborate dinner shared with you,' she said. 'I'd sooner be alone.'

'You are behaving like a sulky child,' he said curtly. 'I thought I had cured you of that tendency and taught you a little to grow up and be a woman.' His hand came to her chin and he forced up her head until all that she saw was his dark face, all the sensuality banished from the lips so that he looked stern and distinguished. His eyes raked over her face, searchingly, taking in the fine-boned contours, the smooth skin, the lips that needed no colour to embellish them, for the power of his kisses still lingered and they had a sort of wild flush against the pallor of her skin.

'You are feeling all right, eh?' He frowned slightly as he studied her. 'Just understand, Persepha, that I did not marry you in order to be another guardian to you.'

'I'm well aware of why you married me,' she rejoined. 'I didn't dwell under the misapprehension that you meant to be kind even before you – you availed yourself of what you bought. At least you found out that Marcus had guarded me well.'

'Yes, *querida*.' His long fingers suddenly ran over the cool contours of her face. 'Are you such a child that you cannot understand what makes men the way they are?'

'I understand what makes you the way you are, *señor*.' She said the word as if she addressed a stranger who meant nothing to her. 'Your arrogance and self-will have never been opposed in any way, so it was rather hoping for a miracle that a mere girl of twenty could fight you and not be beaten down. I hope you enjoyed an un-

51

willing woman in your bed for once. It must have been a new experience for you, for I understand from old Carmenteira that you are *el magnifico* to every other female for miles around.'

'And what am I to you?' he asked, half-mockingly.

'Certainly not magnificent,' she said scornfully. 'You're just my owner, my tamer, who uses a superior physical strength to prove his male superiority. Don't you trust your own charm, Don Diablo? Did instinct tell you that you'd only get me by using force?'

'You had best beware, Persepha,' he said, with soft-voiced menace. 'I may yet decide that my appetite for dinner is less than my appetite for you, for when the fire of anger stirs under that cool disdain of yours, you are more than lovely, and I really don't care a snowdrop in hell what you think of me.'

And with these words he deliberately gripped the neck of her dress and tore it from her with that easy and frightening strength, that ruthless disregard of what she had possessed and clung to in her former life. The shirt of hyacinth blue, and now the honey-brown dress which she had often worn to take dinner with Marcus at Stonehill.

'You – you damned brute!' she gasped, and forgetful of her resolve to remain cool and disdainful, she struck at his face with her hand and then cried out again as he swiftly stayed her hand before it could hit him, almost breaking her wrist in his relentless grip.

'If you want a fight, Persepha, then we'll have one,' he said, and his eyes were devilishly alight as he bent his face to her, holding her forcibly, stripped of her dress and clad only in a pale slip. 'You know how it will end, don't you? Is that what you want? To be again in my arms, helpless and at the mercy of whatever I want of you?'

'I – I'd sooner be dead,' she almost sobbed. 'I utterly

hate you, do you know that? Living with you is like living in hell with Satan!'

'In which case life will never become boring for you, will it, my bad-tempered little cat.' And so saying he marched her to the wardrobe and there he rattled the hangers on the long rail as he took stock of the long gowns and the short ones. He finally selected a gown of mint-green lace, which he handed to her. 'You will put this on,' he said, 'and I will brook no argument. Come, are you going to force me to be your valet, or will you put it on yourself?'

'I notice you say valet and not lady's maid,' she said tartly, snatching the dress from him. 'What a pity it isn't white lace, then you could really pretend that we were bride and groom taking our first starry-eyed supper together.'

'Sarcasm, *querida*, does not become you.' He lounged against the bedpost as she stepped into the dress and he watched her beneath lazily drooping eyelids as she pulled the pale and lovely lace up over her slim body. His eyes followed the movement, and Persepha felt a flush coming into her cheeks. She knew exactly what was going through his mind; he was remembering the look and feel of her in his arms, and when his mouth took on that sensuous curve she knew that in his thoughts he was running his lips over her white skin and her soft contours. Her flush deepened resentfully, for she knew the silky texture of her own skin and how it must feel to a man, especially one so hard and so tanned by the hot sun and the high winds of Mexico.

'I don't think I care for this colour,' she said. 'I'm not terribly smitten with green—'

'It becomes you,' he said, a hand negligently at rest in the pocket of his crisp white jacket, a contrast to his dark superbly cut trousers. 'The colour brings out the soft gold lights in your hair and pays a compliment to your eyes with their little golden glimmers. Do you wish my help with the hooks and eyes?'

'No, thanks, I can manage perfectly well.' Her hands trembled as she hooked up the dress at the side, so that it fitted itself to her waist and her slender hips. In truth it was rather a beautiful dress, but she didn't want to look attractive in it; she didn't wish to like a single thing he had bought her. She went mutinously to the vanity table and there she took up the ivory hairbrush and applied it to her hair. And through the mirror she could see the Don watching her, and it went through her like a knife that he owned her just as he owned this house, all this wonderful carved furniture, these objects of crystal and silver on the table-top.

'Open the little golden box,' he ordered. 'Take out what is inside.'

Persepha pretended not to hear him, but all the same her eyes dwelt in some curiosity on the box, which in itself was a lovely object, with a look about it of being an antique of Mexican design. She concentrated on arranging her hair in a full, soft chignon at the nape of her neck. A style which Marcus had much liked, and which brought a little shadow into her eyes as she thought of him. He had made the demands of a guardian, that she be a good, sweet, obedient companion to him, but he had not been cruel to her, as the Don had been.

She tilted her chin and defied her own reflection, which chose to be a most effective one despite her inward misery. Then her nerves jarred as the Don moved and began to approach her at the mirror. He came and stood tall and intimidating behind her, catching and holding her gaze in the glass.

'Open the little box,' he said again, and his voice had softened in that incredibly menacing way that seemed to

54

play with her nerves as a flame might play with a moth. 'Surely you are curious to see what is in it? It might be an asp for you to put to your breast – who knows?'

'You wouldn't be that merciful,' she said. 'You haven't tormented me enough just yet.'

'Little fool.' His hands slid down the sides of her body and he drew her swiftly against his own hardness, holding her so that they were reflected almost as one in the mirror, her pale green lace shimmering against his black and white, her fairness in startling contrast to his darkness. Her quick fear matched by his lazy amusement.

Then her heart came into her throat as his hands came caressingly to her shoulders and gripped them. 'Was it so very hateful?' he murmured.

She knew what he meant and her entire body seemed to burn and she wanted to hide herself away from him. 'W-what do you think?' she muttered. 'I have bruises all over me, and Carmenteira saw them and looked at them as if they were medals you'd pinned on to me. I'm not used to brutality, but I suppose I shall have to grit my teeth and become used to it.'

'You said you were made of marble,' he mocked. 'Marble doesn't bruise, surely?'

'What do you think this is?' She held out her arm and there against her skin, plum-dark, was one of his marks. 'A tattoo I thought would look rather nice?'

He took her arm in his fingers and bending his head he quite deliberately laid his lips against the bruise. 'A man has only to breathe on you, *querida*,' he drawled. 'I never in my life saw a skin as fine and white as yours. See how swarthy I am in contrast.'

'Like an Indian,' she retorted. 'Isn't it part of your lore to forcibly take the woman whom you marry? To shake her like a rug and tread all over her, just to prove yourself the lord and master?'

He laughed low in his throat. 'You would make a very flimsy rug, *chica*, and I can't recall treading on you.'

'Oh, you know what I mean, *señor*, so don't quibble.' She herself quivered at the tightening of his hands, and the sensual gleam of danger in his dark eyes, seen through his lashes like the flicker of flame. In his hands lay a strength which could have broken her in half, and held to him she had a delicate strangeness, a fair fragility, an appeal to those half-primitive impulses she saw slumbering in his gaze.

'Are you going to quibble about opening that box?' he asked.

'I suppose you've put a trinket in it?' She curled her lip. 'Is it to pay me for services rendered?'

'My girl,' he drawled, 'you are asking for something and I don't know whether it's a spanking or a kissing. Take your choice!'

'I think I'll take the trinket.' She reached for the little box, chased all over with exotic designs in gold; tropic birds and foliage, and tiny weird masks. 'Aztec?' she asked.

He inclined his head and he himself was like an Aztec figure engraved in bronze, his features in hard repose as Persepha lifted the lid of the box and exposed what lay inside. She had known it was a jewel, but she hadn't dreamed it would be so exquisite, so unusual, so breathtaking. Her breath caught audibly and she gazed dazzled at the perfect replica of a dragonfly made entirely from diamonds and emeralds, with claws and jaws of shining gold, the gems so arranged in the spread wings that they seemed to give an illusion of trembling life to the lustrous thing.

'It is pretty, no?'

Persepha gave a start as her husband spoke, for the tiny jewelled eyes of the dragonfly had seemed to catch and hold her own.

56

'Very pretty,' she agreed. 'Are the gems real?'

'Would I give you false ones?' he asked. 'It was designed and made by an old Indian who hunts game in the gorge below the hacienda. When he came to me with the brooch I didn't ask him how he had came by the gems; I could only guess that he either mined them, or murdered to get them. He wished to sell so that he could provide his young daughter with a dowry, and as you remarked earlier today I have a liking for what pleases my eyes, and when I like something I won't be denied. The dragonfly will look well against the lace of your dress, as if from the jungle it had flown to a tender young plant. Pin it just over your heart.'

In this instance Persepha didn't argue with him, for a brief glance at his face showed her that he meant her to have the jewelled dragonfly, and she couldn't deny to herself that it was entirely charming, even though he had intimated that the Indian craftsman might not have come honestly by the gems.

She could feel the tremor in her hands as she took the brooch from the Aztec box, and Don Diablo must have seen that tremor, for quite without hesitation he took the brooch from her fingers and proceeded to attach it to the lace of her dress, just where he had indicated, just above where her heart beat as the living wings of a dragonfly would flutter when it settled on a jungle blossom. Persepha almost held her breath as the Don stood so close to her, his face so serious and intent as he pinned the brooch, his fingers warm against her body. She fought not to be aware of his touch and the memories evoked by the feel of him, and the aroma of him.

She stood very still while the nerves plunged about in her body, and when the brooch was pinned she ran the tip of her tongue around her dry lips. He would expect her to thank him ... but instead he ran his fingers in a light

57

caress down her cheek, and he said, quizzically: 'A small token for being beautiful in my arms, if not willing. As the dragonfly is perfect in all its parts, so are you, little wife. As the dragonfly makes a trembling magic as it flickers through the air, so do you make a magic that flickers through my blood. I wanted you, *querida,* from the moment I saw you at Stonehill, and I have you, have I not?'

'Yes,' she said, almost in a whisper. 'For now, Don Diablo.'

'For as long as I decree,' he said, the arrogance back in his voice. 'And now we will go downstairs, where I wish to introduce you to the more important people who hold positions on the estate. They will be charmed by you, Persepha. You have beauty and dignity when you are not fighting me tooth and claw.'

She walked with him down the curving marble and wrought-iron staircase, and remembered her terror of that afternoon, when he had stormed up those stairs with her in his arms, like some black-haired barbarian who had just snatched for himself a girl to love. Her fingers clenched the iron rail, wrought into lacy patterns, for she had to hold on to something or go toppling headlong down those fateful stairs, to the foot of them where in the graciously tiled and arcaded hall stood a crowd of Mexican people.

It was utterly feudal ... completely unrelated to the world she had known all her life. At Stonehill there had been but a handful of servants, but here at the Hacienda Ruy there were entire families living under the Don's jurisdiction, some with the same blood as he running in their veins.

He was their *hidalgo;* their employer and their godfather. He was all things to them ... but to Persepha he was the husband whom she feared.

CHAPTER FOUR

THE hacienda seemed so high and solitary, so cut off from the kind of civilization to which Persepha was accustomed, that when after breakfast one morning the Don suggested that she take a drive into the town with him she looked astonished. They had risen from the table out on the patio, beyond which rose the bell-tower of the hacienda chapel, a blending of grace and austerity that was so Latin, mixing a love of beauty with a sort of wildness and melancholy. The humming of bees and the tree-shrouded songs of the birds seemed to add to that indefinable air of mystery and passion. Never was there a sunlight so golden, nor shadows quite so black.

Orange flower petals, waxen and lovely, lay scattered on the tiles of the patio. The warmth brought out the tang of the green camphor trees, and there were blue passion-flowers starring the archway where Persepha paused to glance at her husband, her eyes a deep golden-brown as they dwelt on his face. She had wondered why he was dressed so formally in one of those smooth grey suits that fitted him like a glove and gave him such an air of dignity and grave charm.

What a deceptive charm, she thought, when it concealed a man without mercy, to whom she had been married for five long weeks.

'Surely we must be miles from a town,' she said. 'It certainly feels as if we are.'

'As the eagle flies,' he agreed. 'But a swift car can soon cover those miles and I thought you might like to look around the shops and buy things. Candy and records and a few cosmetics. Magazines and books and some perfume. Those incredible oddities dear to the female heart.'

'You must be feeling generous, *señor*.' Even after five weeks of living with him, Persepha still couldn't bring herself to speak to him as if he were her husband; still she thought of him as the tyrant under whose sway she had fallen when brought low by grief and the loss of her home. He owned her, that was all. He took, she never gave.

'Why, because I offer you a shopping trip?' he quirked a black eyebrow and swept those possessive eyes of his up and down her slim figure in a butter-gold dress without sleeves, to the shoulder of which she had pinned the dragonfly brooch. The sun caught the gems and they flashed and burned, and the reason why she often wore it was that it symbolized what lay in her heart ... the wish for flight; the wild hope that one day soon she would be able to get away from the Hacienda Ruy and the man whom the laws of the church compelled her to obey. The gems were real and the brooch could be sold, and that was all she cared. She attached no sentimental value to it, for it had not been given to her out of love.

'I have to go into town on a matter of business and so you might as well come with me,' he said. 'I have to see my lawyer, and I am going to trust you, *querida*, to take a look around the shops and not get any foolish ideas about vanishing. I warn you beforehand that it will be hardly possible, for no one will rent you a car and the nearest railway is beyond those hills.'

He gestured with a lean hand to the distant peaks, smoke-blue and awesome, the high rocky guardians of his kingdom.

'You have earned a trip,' he half-smiled, coming towards her, so that his long, long shadow moved along the sunlit ground. Persepha tensed against the flower-

60

draped archway column, her nerves in a state of clamour before those warm dark hands took hold of her. By now she should have been used to his touch, but still it could arouse her to a state of near-panic, so that she wanted to beat at his shoulders and struggle like a mad thing.

He gazed down at her through his lashes, and there was a mockingly amused quirk to his lips. He studied the curling tendril of hair that clung golden to the side of her neck. 'To be entirely placable is to be entirely boring, *chica*. I have only to touch you and I feel as if I take hold of a young tigress who would like to rip out my eyes. I have an idea! There is a beach near to the town and I think we should swim together. You would like that?'

At the very thought of cool blue water, washing over her limbs, buoyant and relaxing, she trembled like a child who could hardly believe that she was being offered a little kindness after being unfairly punished. 'Do you mean it?' She looked up at the Don with unbelieving eyes, and his answer was a slightly curt laugh.

'Do you have to look at me as if I've just offered you an hour's parole from your prison?' he asked. 'Of course I mean it. You have a swimsuit, eh?'

'I think so.' She couldn't quite remember any more what she had thrown into her suitcase that last day at Stonehill, and she rarely looked at the things he had bought her, merely pulling a dress from a hanger and putting it on, or snatching from a cedarwood drawer some item of lingerie. She covered her body without caring if she looked attractive; she had learned the hard way that to look alluring was to wake the tiger that slumbered in the body and soul of this man, and she would have worn sackcloth and ashes if she could have got away with it.

'Then go and fetch it,' he said. 'And if you will be so

good fetch my trunks from the bottom drawer of the chest in my room. And bring a bath towel, *querida.* I shall be waiting in the car out by the main courtyard.'

He let her go and she sped away into the hacienda, passing Carmenteira as she ran, who was pottering about putting flowers in the big shiny pots in the hall.

Up in her room Persepha opened the wardrobe and pulled out her suitcase which had lain untouched since the night the Don had ordered her to wear only the garments which he had bought for her. She threw back the lid of the case and she stared at all the familiar things that brought back not vivid but curiously grey memories of Stonehill. She fingered the shirts and folded dresses, and gripped the album that held photographs of Marcus and herself taken on those European trips they had enjoyed together. A book of ghosts, she thought. Lost days of dreams and talk in places far from Mexico.

She found her swimsuit at the bottom of the case and drew it out. It was a dark flame colour and in the one-piece style, for Marcus had not approved of the bikini, which had offended his eye with its love of Georgian graciousness.

As Persepha held it up against her she reflected that Don Diablo would probably disapprove of the bikini, and out of sheer perversity she wished that the swimsuit was one of those skimpy garments that just about sat on the hips and covered the breasts with the minimum of material. What a shock for the Don when he saw her so scantily clad in front of other men on the beach; it was bred into his Spanish bones to possess a woman to the exclusion of everyone else.

Anyway, she had been awarded a trip to town, which she had not yet seen, and she must make the most of it. She must hurry or he might change his arrogant mind and drive off without her. She sped into the bathroom for one of the big fluffy towels, and hesitated a moment out-side the door of his bedroom.

On the occasions she had been there she had not gone voluntarily, but had been carried there in his arms, to the enormous couch that filled the octagonal window space overlooking that sheer drop to the gorge. Once there had been white-gold moonlight flooding into the room through the great windows and no experience for her had ever been so out of the world, as if some dark god of natural forces held her in some pagan rite by the light of the moon.

As Persepha entered his room her gaze fell upon the couch, which was covered by an immense brown-black fur, and she gave a shiver of sheer recall as she seemed to feel again the sensual softness of the fur against her skin.

She swiftly turned her gaze from the couch and went to the carved chest that held his clothing. On top of the shining wood lay his hairbrushes backed with tor-toiseshell, his stud-box in leather, and one or two other items of masculine use. His *cigarro* smoke still lingered there, along with the tangy cologne which he used. Across the foot of his bed lay his robe of dark heavy silk, and a leather-handled whip had been carelessly dropped to the floor from his early morning ride around the estate, from which he returned for his session in his steam-room.

He always emerged looking very relaxed, with his black hair ruffled by the steam and a flagrant look of power in his torso and limbs. Clad in his robe he would come and go in her bedroom and bathroom, throwing out orders for the day, and sharing with her a tray of rolls, coffee and jam brought to her by one of the copper-tinted maids who worked in the kitchen. Sprawled on her bed, with its lace and flounces, he always looked outlandishly male, even slightly younger than when he was formally dressed in the evenings.

Persepha opened the bottom drawer of his chest and sorted about until she found the black bathing-trunks ... and something else which she had not expected to find ... the silver-framed photograph of a woman, raven-haired, clad in a silk gown the colour of a geranium, a silk fan spread open in her long white fingers, a smile on her lips that were as luscious as a rose that the warm sun had opened from a scarlet bud. That the photograph was in colour added startling warmth and beauty to the woman's face, eyes, and supple figure. She leaned against a patio column, with the flowered arch above her lovely head. That she was Spanish was evident in her every feature, and in the charmingly flirtatious way in which she held the embroidered fan.

Persepha stood very silent and still and absorbed the woman's Latin beauty, framed by the chaste silver, and kept by the Don among his clothes. Who had she been that he kept such a memento of her? Someone special, for Persepha had never seen any sign of other women he must have known.

'What has the *señora* found that is so intriguing?'

Persepha gave a start that went through her body and she whirled about to see old Carmenteira standing just inside the doorway. The knowing old eyes saw at once the silver-framed photograph in her hands, and feeling as guilty as a schoolgirl caught where she shouldn't be, Persepha swallowed the dryness from her throat.

'The *señor* wished me to find his bathing-trunks ... can you tell me who this is, Carmenteira? She's very beautiful and I just couldn't resist taking a look—'

'The *señora* is curious, eh?' Carmenteira came slowly to Persepha's side and stood looking at the woman in the picture frame. 'Really a Spanish beauty, from her ankles like ivory to her hair like silk. See her eyes and how they sparkle with the joys of life and love? Is the bride of Don Diablo envious of such gaiety, such passion, such allure? Does she see a woman that he might have loved ... really loved as he only desires his white-skinned girl of another race, who turns her eyes when he looks at her, who shrinks from his touch, and trembles at his passion?'

'So she was someone he loved,' Persepha said quietly. 'Where is she now? Do you know?'

'She is dead, señora. Gone from all laughing and all loving these past six years. The Señor Don was inconsolable, do you know that? When it happened he rode off on his most favoured horse and he rode that horse until it fell and had to be finished with a bullet in the brain. He spoke to not a soul for days on end, and at the funeral it was thought that he would throw himself into her grave.'

Old Carmenteira transferred her wise and slightly wicked gaze to Persepha and a jeering look went across her swarthy, wrinkled face. 'How could he love you when he loved such as her? How could he care how he treats you ... you are only the means by which he will get a son for himself, and that's why he seems so fond of your body. She was wine and honey ... you are milk and a dash of bitters. And I speak the truth, and you know it, don't you, señora. I am too old in the ways of men and women not to know what he wants of you.' Abruptly, almost painfully, one of the dark bent fingers prodded Persepha in the stomach. 'Young, fair, healthy, and with a look of breeding about you. Yes, nice young virgins have pretty babies, and he knows it's time for his heritage to be secured. Yes, they always come from sheltered homes, or convents, the brides of his kind. But the women they adore . . . they come from heaven or hell, and they leave their memory like an undying scent.'

And as the old woman's words died away, Persepha, knowing that it was all true, what had just been imparted to her, turned to the chest and returned the framed photograph to its hiding place among the Don's things. Carrying his bathing-trunks, she paused only long enough in her bedroom to collect her swimsuit and the orange towel. He would be growing impatient, and as she hastened down the stairs she wondered why she had an almost shocking impulse to launch herself into space to the tiles of the hall.

She shuddered and ran, making for the outer courtyard, running through the sunlight and shadow to the side of the man who had married her to have a son. She wanted above all to go to town, to see people and shops, and to swim in the sea until she was exhausted.

'I'm sorry,' she cried out as she saw him waiting by the side of the sleek silver car. 'Old Carmenteira wanted to tell me something and she delayed me. Oh, isn't the sun hot!'

'You shouldn't race about in heat such as this, and where is your hat? You will need it!'

'I – I forgot it. It won't matter – I can buy another when we get to the shops.'

As she spoke so breathlessly, and stood there a moment almost swaying, he caught hold of her and looked deep into her eyes. 'You are all nerves, like a netted bird flying madly about in a cage. Is it so wonderful to be going to town for the day?'

'Yes!' She flung back her hair from her brow, which felt hot. 'If you hadn't given me this break, small as it is, I think I'd have gone crazy. What do you think my life is like, here under your roof, watched day and night by you, ordered what to do, what to wear! I'm your thing and all you want of me is—'

She broke off, for to put it into words was to inflict upon herself a form of self-torture. It was awful enough that Carmenteira had painted such a graphic word picture of her place in the Don's scheme of things. Someone desirable enough to breed for him a male child to carry on his name; to inherit his vast lands and his fortune. A woman didn't have to be loved in order to have a baby; all that was needed was the man's passionate, ruthless desire to have his own way.

'A pretty thing, in all truth.' He abruptly bent his head and laid his lips against her brow. 'Get into the car, *chica*, and do try to relax.'

'Will you be driving?' she asked ingenuously.

'Yes.' His look was sardonic. 'You may sit at the back if you wish, away from me. I drive fast and I might unnerve you, as you seem in such a highstrung state since I invited you to go with me.'

With a feeling close to relief Persepha took advantage of his dry suggestion that she sit alone, and when she entered the car she found there were linen covers on the seats to keep the leather from getting hot, and almost as soon as they were out on the highway the air-cooling system began to work and she lay back in her seat and felt the cool air blowing against her closed eyelids. On the seat at her side reposed the swimwear and the towel . . . in her mind lingered the face of a Spanish woman with vivid eyes in love with life.

During that swift drive Persepha's gaze dwelt often on the well-groomed head and broad shoulders of the man seated at the wheel in front of her, and there was a question in her eyes. She had thought him too hard, too careless of feminine feelings to ever really love a woman, yet now she had discovered that he had once loved, and was in all probability the type of man to love only once in a lifetime. It made him seem more human, but at the same time it starkly underlined the position which Persepha held in his life.

She was not loved, and yet she had to accept from him all the various attentions of a husband; she had to submit to his demands whether she desired to or not: she had to live with him until she found some means of getting away from him.

Now more than ever she wanted to get away, and her fingers crept to the brooch that gleamed against her dress and she traced with her fingertips the shape of the wings set with small emeralds and outlined by the white fire of diamonds. If she could find someone to buy it, then all she had to do was sneak her passport and travel documents out of his desk, the massive, many-drawered antique in his office, and she felt confident there was someone on the estate who could be bribed into driving her to the railway. Once she was aboard a train and heading for one of the tourist resorts of Mexico, she would be safe. He surely couldn't snatch her away under the eyes of American and European travellers, who came to this exotic land for the sunshine, the handcrafts, and the history.

The cacti-scattered spaciousness of the landscape was at last left behind and the car headed into the outskirts of the local town, where the houses were colour-washed, with gaily shingled roofs, small orchards, lines of washing hanging in the yards, where small children and livestock ran about together, laughing and squawking and grunting all in a lovely muckiness that made Persepha chuckle to herself as she leaned forward in her seat to watch them as the car drove past.

Don Diablo must have heard the little chuckle she gave, for he threw over his shoulder the remark that she seemed to be enjoying the drive.

'Look at those kids,' she said. 'How do their mothers ever get them clean again?'

'They dump them all together in the wash-tub and pour lukewarm soapy water over them, then they put them out in the sun to dry off.' There was a droll note in his voice. 'Do you find them cute?'

'They're quite beautiful,' she had to admit. 'Such silky brown skins and huge brown eyes; I expect they look like coffee-coloured cupids when they are clean.'

'Yes, Mexican children do have an unspoiled beauty,' he agreed, and this time Persepha caught in his tone of voice a note of meaning that made her heart miss a beat. It was the first time in their relationship that children had been mentioned, and as she stared at the deep peak of hair that cut into the coppery skin of his neck she seemed to feel that he was hinting at what he really wanted of her. And it was true that Carmenteira was old and wise enough to know all about men and women; and to know especially about the master of the hacienda, for she had been here in his mother's time and she had seen him born, and seen him grow up, until he had begun to cast eyes at girls, and had finally loved and lost that radiant Latin beauty in the photograph.

'Do you like children, *señor?*' she asked curiously.

'I find them amusing,' he drawled. 'What of you, *querida?* Would it please you to have a child ... my child?'

Her heart felt as if it turned over this time and her fingers hurt themselves clenching her clutch bag. 'I shouldn't,' she said coldly, 'very much enjoy giving birth to the Devil's imp.'

'*Gracias, mi esposa.* You have a charming way of speaking to your husband at times.' And as he spoke he drove the car into the town centre, towards a lovely old square where other cars were parked, and where they seemed to be looked down upon haughtily by a helmeted stone figure on a horse with its forelegs high in the air.

After leaving the car they crossed the square in the direction of the arcaded shops. Here there was a sound of human bustle and noise as people did their marketing and stood gossiping in the sunshine. Persepha felt suddenly conspicuous, for her hair was so bright and fair in comparison to the brunette women, some of whom toted their shopping baskets like Indians on their dark heads. She by comparison was almost platinum – fair, with a pale skin that made her feel bloodless when she looked at these lusty, coppery females, whose lustrous dark eyes dwelt openly on Don Diablo as he passed them by, a possessive hand beneath her elbow.

Why, she wondered, had he chosen not to marry a woman of his own country? Had he found it impossible to find a substitute for his Latin love, and so had gone to the other extreme and married someone who could never remind him of sparkling dark eyes, shining dark hair, and fingers adept at playing with a fan or clicking the Spanish castanets of the flamenco dance?

He brought her to a halt beneath the long arcade where the shops were bright with exotic window displays; things to wear and objects for the home: adornments and spicy foods: pots and pans and bright fruits.

'You will need money,' he said, and took from his wallet a crisp handful of notes. 'Buy whatever takes your fancy, and especially a sun hat. I shall probably be tied up for the next two hours, but at one o'clock be at the car and we'll go to the Café Valentino for lunch, and then to the beach.'

'Yes, master,' she said, pertly, accepting the money which she handed to her. She glanced at the notes and saw that he had been very generous, but not generous enough that she could bribe anyone to drive her out of his reach.

'What kind of hat shall I buy, one of those with a high crown and a bunch of cherries on the side?'

'Whatever sort of hat, it would suit you.' He gripped her chin and tilted her face to him. 'Don't try and run away from me, *chica*. My arm is a long one, and I hold tenaciously to what is mine. You are mine and you had better know it. All of you, from your hair to your ankles; the flesh and bone of you, the temper and the trembling. My wife, *querida*. The Señora Ezreldo Ruy, who behaves herself with dignity, and appears to have as charming a disposition as she has a charming face and body. These people know me, and they know who you are. You won't be accosted ... unless you invite it, and I warn you not to do so. Do I make myself understood?'

'To the very last syllable, *señor*. I am to be a good girl, and I'm to amuse myself with frivolous things while my lord and master conducts his important manly business.'

They looked silently at each other after she spoke ... the defiance in her eyes warring with the flicker of temper in his. Then all at once his eyelids drooped and that deep line of ironic amusement clefted his brown cheek. 'You are brave among all these people,' he drawled. 'How will your courage be when we are alone again?'

She quaked a little at his words and hated herself for those flashes of cowardice which he induced in her. But he was so strong, so ruthless, and as her gaze flickered back and forth across his shoulders she remembered how they felt in the grip of her hands, smooth and bare and warm as heated copper.

'Oh, I'll be good,' she said, letting her gaze fall away from him. 'I'd hate to see someone beaten up by you. I know your strength, and I know your cruelty.'

'Then so be it!' He spoke crisply and carried her hand to his lips. '*Adios* for now. Be at the car at one o'clock.'

'On the dot,' she promised, and watched him stride tall and purposeful away from her, a distinctive figure in his impeccable grey suit. Persepha sighed, and then turned towards the shops and the diversion of their colour and noise and aroma. She found herself looking at stunning silk shirts in a variety of designs, the kind that would never be seen in England, and which if she still lived there she wouldn't dare to wear. But here where the sunlight was so much a part of the day, from early in the morning till the plum-blue fall of dusk, these lovely bright patterns were appropriate. And she liked the informality of shirts and the feel of them on her figure; she was enamoured of two of these, one with a flame-coloured hibiscus pattern, and the other with moons and stars and curious Aztec patterns against the thin supple silk. She bought them, and then found a market stall selling straw hats, where to her ironic delight there was on display a high-crowned sombrero with a pair of curious-shaped fruits attached to the ribbon of the brim.

After what she had said to the Don, she couldn't resist buying the hat. The trouble was she felt shy about wearing it, and because it was shady beneath the shopping arcades she carried the hat by its brim, and a tiny smile came and went about her lips. There were times when it was a wicked kind of challenge being the wife of the Devil himself. Although there was little dignity in their private tussles, she knew that he was conscious of his position and liked to have an air of masterful and dignified behaviour in front of other people. This hat was for fun and she meant to wear it on the beach, for she was after all an English girl and not that woman in the photograph, with her hair smooth as silk, a creamy flower pinned into her chignon.

About an hour had drifted away, while she wandered and looked at a variety of new and strange things, when all at once Persepha caught sight of a jewellery store. The lustre and glimmer of its windows was not entirely what drew her; she stood there thoughtfully, and her fingers crept again to the brooch pinned to the shoulder of her dress. It would do no harm, surely, if she strolled casually to the counter of the shop and asked the value of the dragonfly brooch. She would then know how much she could expect to get for it ... with abrupt resolve she entered the shop and approached the counter.

For the past hour she had been encountering people with the coppery skins and blue-black hair of Mexico, but to her surprise the young man who came to ask if he could be of service was blond and well-built, with a pair of grey eyes that looked at her with equal astonishment.

'Are you American?' he asked, with a twang in his voice.

'Are you English?' she asked, in unison.

Then they both gave a laugh, which as it died away left a pleased surprise in its wake.

'Oh, you're English,' he said, his eyes smiling at her. 'No doubt in the world about it. That voice, that skin ... English as a cup of tea!'

'Well, I'm not sure how I should take that,' she smiled in return. 'I don't need telling that you're an American ... that twang, that bounce ... American as a cup of coffee!'

Again they laughed together, like two people who had craved the sight of a pale skin, and the sound of English words, whether spoken with a cool incisiveness, or a warm drawl.

'This is the nicest surprise in a long time,' said the young man, and his eyes went slowly over her slim figure in the butter-gold dress that just hinted at tender contours without fully revealing their outline. His gaze slipped up and down her slim white arms, as if he were drinking in the cool, gold look of her. 'I never expected to see a beautiful British girl walk in here like a vision of coolness in this hot land. Are you a mirage, or are you real?'

When his voice deepened on that word 'real' Persepha guessed that he was tempted to reach out and touch her. She would step quickly away if he tried, and she pretended she didn't feel a prick of fear in case, in his tall silent way, the Don appeared and saw another man with his hand upon her.

'I believe I'm real,' she said. 'I never expected to see a Yankee behind the counter of a Mexican jewellery store.'

'It's a living,' he drawled. 'I kind of drifted into it after a bit of an accident ... I used to be a diver for an oil company, sea-oil, you know, and I dived a little too deep one day and got the bends. A friend of mine had this store and offered me the job for a while, until I feel thoroughly fit enough to go back to my old occupation. Once a diver, always a diver. It's like flying; you can never really give it up, even after getting bubbles in your blood, or going into a spin and having an air crash. Crazy, but there you are.'

'Understandable,' she said. 'It must have been a frightening experience for you?'

'I was unconscious at the time – it was the afterwards that was awful.' He looked grim for a moment, and then his good-looking features relaxed into a smile again. 'And what are you doing in Mexico this land of dark wine and golden idols? Are you on vacation?'

'I live here,' she replied, and her figure tensed, and her own smile faltered as the facts of her life came to the surface, causing that sensation that felt like bubbles in her blood. 'My home is quite a few miles away, and I came

74

into town by car this morning, to do some shopping and to have lunch here.'

'Are you alone?' His grey eyes had lighted up when she spoke of lunch, as if he immediately thought of inviting her to take lunch with him.

'I'm afraid not.' Persepha felt a little stab of regret that she couldn't agree to eat a meal with this attractive American. 'I came into town with my husband, who had a business appointment and so left me free for a few hours to wander around the shops. I bought a hat. See!'

But the grey eyes were intent upon her face, and then they wandered to her hands, both of them ringed in the Latin way, one with engraved gold, the other with glimmering rubies.

'You look mighty young to be a wife,' he said. 'I thought it was only in Mexico that the men took their brides from the schoolroom.'

'You're flattering,' she said lightly. 'I left the schoolroom quite a while ago, and I've been married several weeks.'

'Only weeks?' He quirked a blond eyebrow. 'Then by any standards you're still a bride – what is your husband doing, allowing you to wander around alone in a Mexican market place? It's something I'd be wary of doing, knowing how hot-blooded these Mexicans are. I'd be afraid someone would run off with you – a lovely thing like you.'

Persepha flushed slightly, for although she was a girl to whom young men had been paying compliments since the end of her schooldays, in those days she had not been the wife of Don Diablo. It smacked of danger to even hear this young man remark on her looks.

'My husband is too well known for anyone to harm me,' she said.

'I see.' The young man studied the flush in her cheeks

with interest. 'Is he some kind of British diplomat, very respectable and all that?'

'No.' Persepha knew instinctively that she was about to spring quite a surprise on the American. 'My husband is a Mexican Don, one of the most powerful landowners in this part of the world. I don't suppose you've met him, but you've probably heard of him. He's Don Diablo Ezreldo Ruy, and we live in feudal magnificence at his hacienda in the high country—'

There she broke off, for the young American was looking at her with an expression in his eyes that betokened more than surprise. It was a mixture of disbelief and protective anger, as if he would leap the shop counter and rescue her, here and now, from the hands of her Mexican husband.

'He's a despot,' he exclaimed. 'Everyone hereabouts has heard of him, and though word had got around that he'd finally married – why, hell, I for one never dreamed that he'd gotten himself a girl like you! You look as if someone had kept you in a rose garden all your life – they say he has Indian blood in his veins. How come you ever met? I have heard that these guys arrange to have brides straight out of convents – is that how it came about?'

'Almost,' she said, and directly the word was out of her mouth she realized that she had near enough given away the fact that she had been coerced into marrying the Don; that it had not been a love match, a coming together of two people of separate ideologies who yet had to have each other.

'Anyway,' she forced a little laugh, 'I didn't come in here to talk about my private life to a perfect stranger—'

'My name's Gil Howard,' he said at once. 'My home base is Los Angeles, and that's how come I speak quite a passable bit of Spanish, enough to get me by in a Mexican jewellery store. I was married once myself, but it didn't work out – I was always away from home, you know how it is, and in the end Lois my wife found another guy. But apart from that I'm respectable enough, and hearing you call me a stranger makes me realize how much I'd like to be your – friend. You have a first name, of course. I don't have to be formal, do I? *Señora* always sounds so mature to me, and you're just a young thing, and I bet your hair in the sunlight is like spun honey.'

Persepha knew that when he began to speak like that she should have turned on her heel and marched from the store ... but oh, it was so good to meet someone who spoke her language in a voice so different from the Don's. It was such a warm and youthful voice without the meaning accent on certain words, that low sting of the invisible whip, or the sensuous purr of the tiger.

'I should insist that you address me as *señora*,' she said primly.

'But you aren't going to insist, are you?' he grinned.

'Well,' she shrugged, 'what's in a first name in this day and age? Mine is Persepha—'

'Say that again!' His grey eyes glinted, half amused, and half inquisitive. 'Did I hear right?'

'You did, Mr. Howard. My guardian was a classical scholar and he liked the name. It's unusual—'

'Out of this world, honey.' Gil Howard shook his blond head in wonderment. 'How was I to know when I got up this morning that I was going to meet Persephone herself! It's incredible, for the girl is even married to a guy who looks and lives like the Lord of Hades himself!'

That really was too much for Persepha, for it was hitting too close to a nerve for her to let this conversation go any further. Nor could she now ask about the brooch, for he was quick-witted, this American, and he might guess directly that she required to sell in order to buy her passage out of Mexico, away from her dark and lordly husband.

She glanced swiftly at her jewelled wristwatch, yet another gift from the Don which she had been obliged to accept. 'I really must fly, Mr. Howard. My husband isn't the very patient type and he'll be waiting for me. Good-bye—'

'*Au 'voir*, Persepha.' There was a wicked note of laughter in the warm and drawling voice. 'I feel sure we'll meet again, for you and I are a pair of strangers in this land, and we need each other – to talk to.'

'Good-bye,' she said again, and ran.

CHAPTER FIVE

PERSEPHA was out of breath by the time she reached the Don's car ... she had just glanced inside and drawn a breath of relief that he had not yet arrived, when hands closed over her shoulders and she was swung round to face him. He studied her tousled hair and her flushed cheeks, and when his eyes narrowed her heart gave a thump of apprehension. He had a devilish way of knowing everything that went on, and somehow she didn't want him to know that she had met and spoken with Gil Howard. The Don would presume she had been flirting, but it had not been that on her side; it was just that she badly needed a friend in this place that was forsaken of her own English kind.

'You look as if you've been to a jumble sale,' he said drily. 'What in the name of the saints is that?'

Persepha glanced at the hat at which he gestured. 'You said to buy a sunhat,' she reminded him, and that little claw of fear slid away. 'Don't you like it, *señor?*'

He had never yet reproved her for being forever formal with him, and with a quirk of his eyebrow he took hold of the hat and tinkered with its adornment of the two orange-coloured fruits. 'The object looks rather like a phallic symbol,' he drawled. 'But I don't imagine that it struck you that way, eh?'

Her flush deepened at his dry words and the wicked glint in his eyes. 'No! I merely thought it a rather amusing hat. Aren't you going to let me wear it, then?'

'My *chica*, I am not that tyrannical in your estimation, am I? Nor so deprived of a sense of humour? If you wish

79

to wear the absurd thing, then by all means wear it – on the beach.'

He handed her into the car and they drove to the Café Valentino, which was a colourful restaurant near the sea-front, its parasoled tables set on a plage above the wash of the ocean itself, where a fine white beach ran to the water's edge, a pale contrast to the warm blue tint of the ocean.

This was the kind of place which appealed to Persepha, and she couldn't help but ask herself why Don Diablo was putting himself out to please her today. She shot a curious glance at him as they took their seats, and when his sardonic eyes met hers, she glanced away again. After their five weeks together was he hopeful that she was already to give him the one thing he really wanted of her? In the smooth grey material of his suit, which was such a contrast to his tawny darkness, he looked every inch the *hidalgo*, the *muy hombre* of intense virility and determination. He had told her that he admired the fighting spirit of the British, and that she supposed was what he wanted in his son; the ruthless and conquering Latin blood intermingled with the unconquerable spirit of her own nation.

It was quite something to be desired, she admitted to herself, but where did the love come in? A child should be born of love, not of arrogant ambition on the father's side. A child should evolve from an absolute melting together of two people passionately attached, and as her fingers clenched around the glass of cool pineapple juice which had been brought to her, she prayed to whatever gods would listen, here in this land both pagan and intensely religious, that she would not have the Don's child.

Long ago, or so it seemed, she had thought that if she ever married and had a child she would like to call him Marcus. But in those days she had not envisioned this kind of marriage ... in those idle moments in the deep window-seat of her bedroom at Stonehill she had youthfully hoped that whoever married her would cherish her as Marcus always had.

'And what else did you buy?' The Don's deep voice broke in on her reflections and she gave a start and looked at him with wide eyes in which that distant dream seemed to shatter, or that was the illusion as the dappled shade of the parasol played across her face, the soft sea wind playing with the scarlet fringes.

'Oh, a couple of shirts to wear informally about the hacienda,' she said. 'The patterns are really eye-catching.'

'Are they?' He took a long sip at his *pisco sour*. 'Is it your intention to catch my eye with them?'

'No – what I mean is – they're just for casual wear.' She bent her head to her drink and drew the juice deeply up through the straw and felt it flow cool and sweet down her dry throat. 'The shops here are filled with bright and attractive goods. Your people are clever with their hands, aren't they?'

'Very much so, and they are your people now, *querida*. You and I are one flesh, or do you still think of yourself as held against your will, and have dreams of escaping from me?' Though he spoke lazily, there was an intent look in his eyes as they dwelt upon her face, with its smooth skin, finely-boned features, and wide-spaced eyes into which a little gold had spilled from her shining hair. A glint of possessiveness came into the Don's expression, and he suddenly leaned forward and his lips seemed to be edged as if with steel.

'One flesh, *amiga*, do you hear me?'

'I hear you,' she said, tensely. 'I don't doubt for one moment that all you care about is the flesh that you like to see in silk and valuable jewels. It excites your eye to see your living possession adorned for you ... there must be a touch of the Moor in you, *señor*. Will you choke the life out of me if I ever seem to stray, like poor Desdemona?'

'I would not advise you to test my temper and tolerance in that direction, Persepha. As you say, I place value on the virtue of my wife, and one of the great moments of my life was finding you so utterly virtuous.'

And when he said that it was as if for vivid seconds this sea café vanished and in its place was the perfumed luxury of her bedroom at the hacienda, with the slide of silk beneath her as with lean hands that brooked no refusal, no amount of fight, the Don made her submit to him.

'It was one of the dark moments of my life,' she flung at him, her voice a low quiver, her eyes hating him for bringing alive that memory, 'when I found I had married a monster!'

'My dear,' he laughed softly, 'do you spend time each day finding new names to call me? No, don't answer my question! I can see that it causes you no effort to find these charming *noms de guerre*. Well, at least they are honest and not the honeyed endearments of a woman who only pretends to be in love. With you, *amiga*, I know where I am.'

'Do you?' she said, and she gave him a look which she purposely meant to be provocative. 'I shouldn't bank on that, *mi esposo*. Still waters are said to run deep.'

'And the British are deep, eh? Partially submerged like icebergs.' As he spoke he began to eat the delicious trout which had been placed in front of him by the silent-footed waiter. He squeezed lemon, added pepper, and smiled slightly.

'Yes,' she retorted, 'and icebergs can be dangerous, *señor*. You have heard of the *Titanic* and how it was sunk even as it proudly flaunted its strength and grace.'

'You know, *vida mia*, you are picking up the Latin fondness for wrapping a dagger in a piece of silk. Latin roots do join those of the Moor, and through the Moor they are buried in the sands of biblical days, and the parable was always a favourite style of expression, then as now. Beware, *chica*, or you might become impregnated with our ways.'

'Heaven forbid!' she rejoined, and she flinched at the word which he used so deliberately. 'I should hate to become cruel and self-willed, with nothing in my heart but ambition.'

'What would you know of what is in my heart?' He buttered a small hunk of brown bread. 'You have never taken the trouble to find out. You suppose that I carry a piece of concrete in my breast, don't you?'

She glanced up from her plate and regarded him with cool eyes. 'I know that you have no real feeling in your heart for me. I'm just a shape which appeals to you; a structure of skin and bone that you treat like a filly who dislikes the halter. You've exerted all your rights as my owner, but if you think I'm going to – to like you for it, then you can think again.'

'I am thinking, *chica*, and at no time can I recall ever asking you to like me. This is very good trout, eh? Quite excellent. You see, I like this trout and I eat all but the bones, but I wouldn't dream of sharing my life with a trout.'

Despite herself, and all that she shrank from in this ruthless man, he had a dry sense of humour that Persepha was not proof against. She wanted to laugh aloud at his remark and had to bite her lip in order to control the urge. She wouldn't, she swore inwardly, give him the satisfaction of having amused her.

He glanced up from his food and she felt the knowing

83

flick of his eyes, and from under her lashes saw his lean fingers reach for his glass of pale gold wine.

'Do give way or you'll choke,' he drawled. 'Do you think, Persepha, that I don't know something about you after these weeks of ours together? You enjoy a joke, and you like it to be a little earthy, and do you know what that proves?'

'No, you tell me, *señor*. You're the authority on women ... of that there isn't a scrap of doubt.'

'It means, *querida,* that you have the makings of quite a woman, and this I believe is a characteristic of the cool blonde of Northern shores, with her outward look of hauteur and reserve. She has burning a little flame inside her and when it really leaps it burns away all inhibition, all discretion, all the ice with which she guards it. It is very intriguing, this little flame of love in the ice maiden.'

'Love?' Persepha laughed now, and scornfully. 'If you spoke of hate, then you'd be nearer the mark. Has a woman ever said to you before, Don Diablo – *I hate you?*'

Between them, after she had spoken, there hung a silence so intense that the sounds of other diners, their chatter and the tinkling of their cutlery, was suddenly over-loud. Persepha herself was gripped by a tension into which each small sound erupted like a shock-wave, and she watched with a kind of fascination beyond fear as the Don's fingers clenched around the stem of his wine glass until she felt certain the pressure would crack the glass. But these were sturdy café glasses and not those fine antiques from which they drank at the hacienda. One of those beautiful things would have gone to smithereens in his hand, for the knuckles stood out whitely against the tawny skin.

'Again you are brave in company,' he said, and there was that in his voice which promised retribution when they were alone, of the kind that she fought against with such spirit only to be defeated by his superior strength of body, his ruthless resolve to have his own way despite her struggles, her use of tooth and claw, and words she hadn't dreamed she had picked up from those gambling companions of her guardian. She had called him more than a devil, and that word was in her eyes right now, flung at him across the table of a crowded restaurant.

He inclined his dark head in mocking acceptance of what she silently called him.

'And what will you have for dessert, something sweet?' he asked, the very essence of sarcasm in his voice. He snapped his fingers for the attention of their waiter, and as Persepha sat dipping her fingers in the little bowl of water to which a rose petal had been added, she noticed from under her lashes the way a trio of women at a nearby table were staring at her husband.

They were Latin women, but so smartly dressed that they were probably the wives of officials here in town. Their eyes held that warm Latin appreciation of an attractive male, and there was no way that Persepha could deny the Don's sensual appeal to every female eye but her own. The way his skin gleamed like warm copper against the white silk of his shirt and the grey of his suit. The way his eyes drooped lazily, their true expression partially concealed by his lashes. The way his shoulders promised an overriding strength in the embrace of man and woman.

Gil Howard had said that the Mexicans were hot-blooded, but the Don was never going to make her blood boil with anything other than temper. Oh, she'd be such a shrew that he'd regret mightily the day he ever set eyes on her ... she'd never look at him the way those women were looking!

Scorn made a cold mask of her face when one of the

women, clad in a dress the colour of purple lilac, managed to catch the Don's eye. She looked directly at him and her eyes were twin pools of dark glimmering invitation. Out of sheer curiosity Persepha then glanced at her husband to see his reaction to that open signalling of a woman probably bored by her own husband and on the lookout for an affair with someone else's.

Don Diablo was looking back at the woman and his face had that bronze Aztec chiselling that always sent a little shiver running through Persepha. So might one of the Aztec lords have looked as he raised his whip and brought it down across the skin of a slave.

With eyes as cold as jet he out-stared the woman, until all at once she gave a rather shrill laugh and returned to her gossiping. But her olive skin was flushed and Persepha realized that something in the Don's look had made the woman feel as cheap as a harlot on offer in the market place. With just a look he had taught her a lesson, and as if to underline it he reached lazily for Persepha's gold-ringed hand ... *this is mine,* the gesture seemed to indicate. *This girl who looks at no other man, and is even nervous of my touch.*

'Never,' he said to her, and his tone of voice was deeply harsh and inexorable, 'never become like that woman over there. If you ever do, then the story of the Moor and Desdemona will be re-enacted, I promise you.'

'Oh?' Persepha felt his touch on her fingers like a warm brand; a threat and a caress in the hard fingertips. 'Don't you find her awfully attractive? So Latin and dark-eyed, so curvaceous and willing? You do surprise me, *señor.* I should have taken her for your type.'

At these words his fingers tightened to the point of pain, but Persepha strove not to wince, and was only released when the waiter came with their sweet, a de-

lectable salad of passion-fruit, grapes and sliced banana
with a bowl of the thick cream that Mexican cooks were
so adept at whipping up and which tasted heavenly, even
to Persepha who hated to admit that anything provided
by the Don was less than bearable.

She couldn't help but enjoy the salad and cream with a
delicate greed, and all the time she sensed the Don watching her with a curious intentness.

'You are in excellent appetite today, *chica*,' he remarked. 'Is it the sea air, I wonder? Or could there be
some other reason?'

He could mean only one thing, though she wanted to
say scornfully that she'd rather be put to death than have
to carry his child, she kept her painful fury reined in tight
against her breast. She looked at him with blank eyes, as if
she didn't comprehend his meaning and had no idea that
he longed for her to be pregnant with his son and heir.

'I'm just a pig for cream,' she said lightly. 'This fair
hair of mine is just hair, you know, not a halo. I have my
greeds just as you have yours, *señor*.'

'*Touché*,' he drawled. 'You have a sharp little tongue
and should have been named Kate, except that I prefer
the name you were given. It has a rare quality just like
you, *mia*.'

'You mean that it has a fateful one,' she corrected him,
her small white teeth crunching a big blue grape. 'I'm
named after Persephone, as well you know, my own dark
lord, and though your hacienda may not be quite like
Hades, it feels like it to me.'

'You find nothing there that pleases you?' He spoke in
a dry tone of voice, as if he well knew her feelings with
regard to his home. 'No beauty in its gardens, no pleasure
in its water-walks, no delight in its patios or its rooms? I
should say there was far more to please the senses at the

hacienda than I saw at Stonehill. It seemed grey and grim to me.'

'Stonehill was my home,' she rejoined, giving him a resentful look. 'I loved it, which is more than I can say for the Hacienda Ruy. It's just a gilded prison as far as I'm concerned.'

'And I your jailer, eh?' He ordered coffee when the waiter came to collect their dessert dishes, and also asked if they had a certain brand of cigar. A box of the cigars was brought almost at once, and Persepha watched silently as the Don selected one and rolled it between his lean fingers in order to test the crispness of the leaf. A light was supplied by the deferential waiter, who when he brought their coffee also brought a dish of bonbons, delightful, almost oriental confections, some of nougat, some of chocolate and others of real candied fruit. A slight smile touched the waiter's swarthy face as he glanced at Persepha, who in her sleeveless dress, dappled by the softly moving shadows of the parasol, looked very young, and very fair in contrast to the dark, powerful figure of the Don, who was so obviously her *padrone*.

'Sweets to the sweet.' The Don pushed the bonbon dish towards her after the waiter had gone. 'Come, *chica*, you said you were feeling greedy and the candy does look inviting.'

'Are you hoping to fatten me up?' She spoke lightly, but couldn't quite meet his eyes as she took a piece of nougat and popped it into her mouth. 'Spaniards as a rule like their wives to be plump and I don't quite meet that specification, do I? In fact, *señor*, I often wonder why you chose to marry a woman who obviously has no affection for you, and barely any respect—'

'Respect?' He took her up sharply then, and flicked ash from his cigar with an impatient movement. 'I certainly don't ask for the schoolgirlish affection which you gave to

88

that guardian of yours, but I do demand that you respect your position as my wife. What is private between us is of no concern to the world at large, but when in public you will conduct yourself as a lady, with your sharp little claws sheathed and your language restrained. I sometimes wonder if Marcus Stonehill was the correct sort of person to have charge of a young, impressionable girl. His household was entirely male, and I understand at times a veritable gambling den. It's a wonder he didn't try to make a pseudo-boy of you.'

'I wish he had!' Persepha stirred her coffee so fiercely that most of it flew over the edge of the cup into the saucer. 'I wish he'd taught me how to earn my living as a card sharp, then I wouldn't be under your authority! Yes, Marcus liked to gamble, but he never imbued me with the fever for it. He kept me out of that side of his life.'

'How innocent of you to say that,' the Don drawled. 'I think, *querida*, that he used you as a small white mouse enticing in the tomcats – ah, if you aim that bonbon dish at me in public, then you had best beware of me in private.'

'You – you really are a devil!' Her face actually whitened as she looked at him, fear and distress burning in her eyes. 'But if you think you can turn me against the memory of Marcus, then you're out of luck. I knew his faults and his virtues, and funnily enough I loved him for both. I only hate you and I see no virtue in you at all – unless it is that you treat your peons with more courtesy than you treat your wife!'

'Don't raise your voice,' he cut in, and now his eyes were glittering with that icy fury she had induced in him once or twice before, which had sent her running from him like a scared young animal, seeking some means of escape but finding only a place to hide, once in the huge kitchen of the hacienda, where she had grabbed an onion and a knife and to the utter amazement of the girl working there had proceeded to strip the vegetable to bits, tears raining down her face, both fear-induced and onion-induced.

But here in the restaurant there was nowhere to go, unless she rushed pell-mell among the crowded tables and made a spectacle of herself. She tossed her hair and glared back at her husband.

'If you wanted a cowed object for a wife, then you came to the wrong shop when you chose me, *señor*. I'm a person in my own right – not just a breeding machine!'

It was out . . . spoken . . . the blade had been twisting in her ever since that encounter with Carmenteira in his bedroom that morning. God, she was but twenty, and life had ended if all she had to live for was to produce the son and heir of a man who felt no real love for her.

'This conversation has gone far enough.' The Don's face was dark and thunderous as he beckoned the waiter and settled the bill. He left a generous tip, and then taking Persepha's elbow in a painful grip he led her from the café, out into the brilliant sunlight where the sea and the sands made a dazzling image. Persepha saw it all as through a blur, and when she blinked she was surprised to feel the cool moistness of tears on her eyelids.

She walked silently with him to the car, for she thought they were going back to the hacienda. Instead he reached inside for the swimsuits and the towel, and for the high-crowned straw hat which had so amused him earlier on. 'It will be hot on the beach,' he said.

'Do you still want to go?' She spoke diffidently. 'It doesn't matter to me if we go – home.'

'Don't be a child, and take this absurd thing. *Por deus*, if you think I'm going to be deprived of a dip in the ocean because we've crossed foils and drawn a little blood, then you can think again. Sit in the car if you don't wish to join me on the beach. Suit yourself!' He began to stride away from her in the direction of the rough stone steps that led down from the plage to the sands. Persepha stared after him, and then her nostrils quivered as a gush of aromatic sea air blew into her face. Oh, to hell with it! She'd swim and swim until she felt so beaten that she was numbed to the reality of things. To hell with him, with his high and mighty swagger and his black head held like a conquering hero!

When Persepha reached the sands she found that the Don had hired one of the beach huts that stood in a colourful line along the dried white tideline, where the water didn't reach when it came in. She hung about kicking at the sand until he emerged from the hut in his bathing-trunks, a strip of black against his lean hips, baring his torso to the strong neck, his legs long, strong and hard as he strode past her to the sea, where it creamed in and whispered seductively. He went right in to his waist and then struck out, his arms glimmering like wet copper.

The whisper of the water was too much for Persepha and she made a dash for the hut and was soon out of her clothes and stepping into her swimsuit. She pulled the dark-flame material up over her slim contours and her white skin, and taking her hair in her fist she tied it with a piece of string which she found in her bag. She ran on bare feet through the warm velvety prickle of the sand and gasped with sheer pleasure, grasping at an illusion of girlhood again as she plunged into the buoyant water and felt it like a vibrant caress against her limbs, and then her body, until she was striking out with both arms.

There was a voluptuous pleasure in being in the sea again; she had always liked to swim since being introduced to the joy of it at an early age by Marcus. She let the sea soothe away her cares, and those bruises of emotion that didn't fade so quickly as those inflicted by a cruel hand. She closed her mind to everything but the enjoyment of the moment, and didn't look around to see the dark head of her husband bobbing on the blue water. She wanted to pretend that she was entirely alone; her own person and not one who was subject to the orders and the demands of a man who aroused in her such antagonism and wilful temper. Marcus wouldn't know her for the pliant, humorous, obedient girl whom he had reared in his bachelor establishment. She would have become a stranger to him with her wild eyes, her flashes of fury, her bursts of hatred. She believed he would have been shocked, for he could not have visualized that she would see in Don Diablo not a rich protector but a ruthless predator, driven by dark currents in his blood.

She was swimming easily, and loving the water that was neither tepid nor too cool. She turned on her back and did the back-arm crawl, slitting her eyes against the burning blue of the sky above her. Everything was so peaceful that she could almost believe that the Don had gone under and drowned ... suddenly she felt curious and looked around her, but there was no sign of him. No dark head could be seen against the blue swell of the water, and a most curious spasm seemed to grip her deep in her stomach.

Had her prayer to the pagan gods been answered? Had he sunk silently and forever out of her life ... and then she gasped and cried out as a swift lean shape swam up out of the very depths, or so it seemed, and grabbed hold of her with a strong, wet, golden arm.

'We have the sea to ourselves,' he chuckled. 'Every other lazy soul is taking siesta ... you swim well, *chica*. You don't flounder about, or fear to get your hair wet. If only you had this same kind of fearless enjoyment in my arms, eh?'

She looked into his wet face creased by his amusement in having startled her, and she wriggled in his grip
like a slim red eel. He had come at her like a shark and
her nerves were still in a tumult . . . 'I thought you had
drowned,' she said. 'Wishful thinking!'

'What sinful thoughts for a wife to be having,' he
mocked. 'My dear, you don't get rid of me as easily as
that; with my Indian blood I not only swim like a fish
but I'm tough as whipcord.'

'Don't you mean a shark?' she asked sweetly. 'Silent,
swift and lethal as that brute of the ocean.'

'Did you think that was what had hold of you?
Further out they hang about the reefs where they fish,
but they rarely come into the bay itself, for it's deep
and clean, with no refuse in it. That was a local law
which I helped to impose, that this bay and its beach
were to be kept in immaculate order for the benefit of
those who wished to swim in some kind of comfort.
Some years ago we had a bad outbreak of the polio
disease in this area, caused by the murky condition of
the bay water, but now they are clean and safe, and
beautifully buoyant, eh?'

She had to agree with him, and in a way she was
unsurprised that he had been influential in making the
bay such a beauty spot, to which the inhabitants of this
town could come in their leisure time to swim in safety
and to enjoy a beach unpolluted by human refuse.

'It was good of you,' she said, 'to put yourself out for
other people. Polio is a very awful disease—'

'Yes.' He spoke shortly, and then gestured at the
beach that lay a shimmering strand of white-gold about
half a mile from where they were, she in the half-circle
of his arm. 'Would it be an awful blow to your male
ego if I actually got the better of you?' she asked.

'Who knows?' he said. 'Shall we put it to the test?'

He released her and at once she struck out for the beach and swam as she had never swum before, putting her entire effort into the attempt to beat him. If only she could! If only by some miracle she could prove that she wasn't a creature so much weaker than he, whom he could reduce to a helpless heap of womanhood, biting her lips to stop herself from pleading with him, but unable to keep the imploration out of her eyes.

When she flung a glance to the side of her, there he was swimming without effort, with strong easy movements of his coppery arms. She saw the glimmer of his white teeth and knew that the devil was just pacing her and that if he so wished he could have outdistanced her at any time he pleased.

In a sudden fury, she kicked water in his face, and as suddenly went under the water in her temper, gasping, choking, and near enough drowning until strong arms caught her and swam the remaining yards to the beach with her, where she was lugged to the dry sand like so much flotsam and dumped there.

A stream of Spanish followed this inelegant action, such fluent invective that Persepha could only guess at its meaning. She choked and coughed and grimaced at the grains of sand all over her wet legs and arms.

'Little fool,' he concluded in English. 'One day you will go a little too far with your childish and foolish actions. Why don't you grow up?'

That he was absolutely in the right to be angry with her was added fuel to Persepha's mortification. 'You're the supreme adult, aren't you, *señor*? You've never done anything foolish – or so you think. The biggest fool-thing you ever did was to make me marry you ... make me come to a country I hardly know ... make me give in to you because I just haven't the strength to fight you. I can only hate your arrogance—'

'That theme is becoming a bore,' he snapped, standing above her like dark justice personified, the water streaming from his body and falling on to Persepha, his bare feet deep planted in the sand. 'You say the word hate so often, *mia,* that it's beginning to lose its sting.'

'So it did have a sting?' she butted in, pushing at her bedraggled hair from which the string had come loose, so that it made an untidy swallowtail down her back. The flame material of her swimsuit clung to her body and she wanted unbearably to get out of it and to rub off all this gritty sand with the towel which had been left in the beach hut.

'I have never,' he said slowly, 'ever permitted from anyone an iota of the insolence that I have taken from you, and the time is rapidly coming to strip you of some of that temper—'

'By breaking my spirit with your whip?' she cut in. 'As if I'm some kind of wild mare that you bought who needs chastising?'

'I don't need to use a whip on you, *querida.*' And suddenly as his voice dropped, he followed suit and was kneeling over her recumbent figure and raking the wet black hair out of his eyes. He had acted so quickly, with such a supple, animal discipline, that Persepha was made captive in the arc of his strong legs before she could roll out of his way.

'Don't!' she gasped.

'Don't?' he mocked. 'Who is going to stop me? Everyone else is at siesta and you and I have an empty beach entirely to ourselves. You can scream, struggle, bite and claw, and bring about your own exhausted defeat more quickly than I can. Come, my dear, let's have our usual wrestling bout before the main tournament—'

'Oh, go to hell,' she said helplessly, and for once she lay supine as he leaned closer to her, until his skin was searing hers with its hard warmth, and she closed her eyes and clenched her teeth as she felt his lips drifting across her throat.

'Ugh, sand grains!' he muttered, and the next instant he had leapt upright and was pulling her with him. His eyes were narrowed and flickering as he gave her a slap across the rump and told her to go and rub down and make herself more presentable. 'Though I will say,' he held her a moment, those devil-eyes playing over her, 'that there is almost nothing more delightful than the disorder of a woman, when she isn't prickly with sand and temper. Run along, little sand-cat, before I change my mind and decide to brave the grit as well as the claws.'

'Sybarite!' she flung at him, only after he had let go her arm and she was able to flee quickly away to the beach hut, her backside in the flimsy material of her swimsuit still stinging from his slap.

Once inside the hut she quickly slid the latch into place, and only then did she feel it was comparatively safe to strip off and rub down with the big towel.

A swim with Marcus had been followed by a blissful laze on the sands, body and nerves in a state of relaxation ... but right now she was as strung up as a cat, jumping at the slightest sound, and relieved when she had zipped her dress and straightened it on her hips.

Darn that man ... he was so deliberately provoking that he made her behave like an ass. Why couldn't she keep her vow to be cool and dignified, instead of flying off the handle and giving him the satisfaction of getting the better of her in one of those undignified tussles.

She combed her hair until it was free of sand and looped the damp, shining tail around itself at the nape of her neck. She then felt a little more composed when she stepped out of the beach hut, and with her nose in the air she walked past the Don who was lounging against a palm tree, his bathing-trunks a bar of black against his sun-gold skin, a single glance at him enough to recall the feel of that skin against hers, so close that not even the sunlight could slip between them. Clad like that he had an untamed look about him, a flagrant masculinity that made her turn her eyes away from him.

'It's all yours,' she said. 'Shall I go and wait at the car?'

She knew, as he guessed, that she was apprehensive of being reached for again and brought close and helpless to that hard, tigerish body of his.

'No, stay here,' he said. 'I shan't be more than a few minutes.'

He vanished into the hut, but he didn't latch it as she had, and she stood there watching the long shining scrolls of water being rolled inevitably towards the beach by the turning tide. She glanced at the sky and saw that a golden glow was creeping into the blue and she realized that the day was starting to die a little.

And then her pulses gave a little bound as she saw the figure of a man making his way from where the plage steps led down to the sands. He was swinging a towel and a swimsuit in his hand, and as the sun touched his hair and made it gleam, that pulse start of Persepha's told her the identity of the strolling figure.

'No!' she wanted to cry out. 'Don't come to me ... don't speak ... don't recognize me!

But of course he did. '*Señora!* This is great!' The twang of his American voice rang out in the stillness, which a moment ago had been broken only by the sound of the sea as it washed forward, and then away again.

Ignore him she couldn't, and despite the closeness of the beach hut, and the quick ears of the Don, she had to respond to Gil Howard ... brazen it out,

'Hullo, Mr. Howard. Are you going in for a swim before the tide comes all the way in?'

'Sure. This is my favourite time of the day, with honest graft behind me and the pleasures of the evening ahead of me.' He loped across the remaining yards of sand that separated them and when he drew close he looked down at her with that flash of quick admiration in his grey eyes. 'I can see that you've been in the sea. You look like Undine right now, all sea-washed and sort of ethereal.'

'Please,' she lowered her voice, her imploring eyes directing his attention to the beach hut where the Don was dressing. 'Don't say things like that – my husband wouldn't understand—'

'Oh, I get it!' Gil Howard gave her a knowing wink. 'So you've been swimming with the Spanish spouse. Say, poor kid, you're all tense and would like me to make myself scarce! Is he that kind of a husband, then? Has a rule about his *esposa* keeping strictly out of contact with other men, keeping to him alone and abiding by all his commands? Say, that must be hell for you!'

'It will be hell for you if you don't *vamos*,' she rejoined, and despite her edginess, and her wish that Gil Howard would depart before the Don saw him, she had to return that quizzical smile which he was slanting down at her.

'Your wish is my command, fair lady. Any hope on earth that we might meet again – alone?'

'None,' she said quietly. 'Please go before he sees you!'

But she spoke too late, for in that instant the door of the beach hut swept open and there was the tall figure of her husband, looking overpoweringly tall on the steps of the hut, grey-clad, his brows in a black bar above his penetrating eyes. Then he came down the steps and even the informality of the towel and the trunks in his hand couldn't detract from his look of the forbidding Latin husband to whom his wife was forbidden to all other men ... even in friendly conversation.

Gil Howard gave him a single comprehending look, then he strolled casually on, to all appearances a passerby who had paused to chat up the English girl who stood presumably alone on the beach. Persepha breathed a little sigh of relief. She hadn't wanted to introduce the two men ... she realized, with a quick beat of her heart, that she wanted Gil Howard to be her secret. Someone she knew and could, perhaps, trust to help her when the time came.

'Was that *hombre* annoying you?' The Don frowned down at her.

'Not really,' she said, forcing a smile to her lips. 'You know what young men are. He was just being friendly—'

'You mean he was trying to pick you up?' The Don's lips were so thin they seemed to give a cutting edge to his words. 'Why didn't you call out for me – or did you enjoy the encounter? I notice he wasn't a young Mexican.'

'No, he might have been English or American – anyway, *señor,* let's forget him. He hasn't damaged my reputation as your wife – there wasn't time for that.'

'Be careful, Persepha.' Hard fingers closed over her shoulder, letting her feel their pressure against her fine bones. 'I would never tolerate any kind of behaviour from you that was some form of retaliation against me. I'd never want you to sink to the level of using another man to get even with me – I'd sooner you used a knife.'

'*Mi esposo,* don't tempt me.' She looked away from him, unable to endure any longer the hard glitter of his eyes. She gazed instead at the fading gold of late afternoon, the deepening shadows on the gilded scroll of the sea on the turn, to whose rustling had been added the crying of seabirds. Some long fishing boats were gliding in, manned by barefoot boys, painted prayers on the prows as they reached for the sands. The sea wind combed tendrils of hair from her brow, and her eyes reflected a great stream of sunset fire across the westering sky.

By her side the Don suddenly quoted some lines in Spanish, and because he spoke them slowly she made them out.

'When the fire goes out, the ashes retain the heat.

When the love flies away, the heart retains the pain.'

As the sunset burned and there came the brilliant afterglow, Persepha thought again of that photograph in the Don's room at the hacienda ... was that the love he was thinking of ... was there still pain in the memory of it, which the dying beauty of the sun recalled for him?

They turned from the sea and walked to the steps that led up to the plage, and Persepha had the conviction that somewhere along the beach Gil Howard was watching their departure. It may have been this that made her careless, for as she mounted the steps the heel of one of her shoes caught in a crack and she stumbled, catching at the Don for support. Instantly his hard arm swept around her.

'Be careful, *querida*! I shouldn't want you to fall and hurt yourself.'

No, she thought resentfully. I have to be kept in one piece in order to produce the *hidalgo's* heir!

'I'm all right.' She jerked free of his arm and hurried to the car, where on the drive home she sat alone in the back, shrouded in a sense of gloom, intensified as the night deepened and fell. The lanterns were alight in the courtyard when they drove in through the gates of the hacienda, and Persepha quickly opened the car door and made her way into the house ahead of her husband. She wanted to be alone with her forlorn thoughts ... it hurt a lot more than she cared to admit that there was no one who loved her just for herself.

Marcus had cared for her because she resembled his beloved Daisy, whose portrait now hung in Persepha's bedroom. The Don exulted only in her virtue and her fair looks ... those were his requirements for the mother of his son. She mustn't damage either of them, and as she rushed upstairs to her room she thought of Gil Howard swimming all alone, and she recklessly hoped that she would see him again, when the Don wasn't around to make friendship seem like a clandestine affair.

CHAPTER SIX

WHEN Don Diablo told her that he had to go away for about a week, Persepha could hardly contain or hide the relief that she felt, and the sense of being given a holiday from his ever watchful eyes.

'I can see that you're pleased that business calls me away,' he said dryly. He then told her that he was flying to the Argentine where he was to negotiate a beef-breeding deal with one of his all-powerful fellow Dons. 'You could come with me,' he added. 'If you wish. I am also buying a stallion and some mares, one of which will be your very own riding horse, so you could make your own choice.'

For a brief moment she felt tempted by the prospect of the journey, but even more ardently she wanted to be free of his sway for a while, and to perhaps augment her friendship with Gil Howard.

'While you're away, *señor*, may I have the use of your car?' she asked. 'Juan Feliz can drive me into town to see the shops, for it does make a break from being in the heart of the country. Please?'

He quirked an eyebrow at the softening of her voice. 'You are being very persuasive, *chica*, and therefore you make me wonder if I would be wise to leave you alone for a week.'

'Alone?' Her heart drummed a warning that she tread carefully if she was to win her reprieve or she'd be snatched back again into his possessive arms. 'I'm sure Juan Feliz would be given your strict orders not to let me stray.'

'True,' he drawled. 'I never asked, but you don't drive yourself, do you, Persepha?'

He looked at her with narrowed eyes, searching her face which she schooled into a bland mask. Though she had never acquired her driving licence, she had taken lessons from Marcus, who had had a way of teaching her the odd accomplishment, the skill with cards being the only thing he had not taught her in his fond and faintly cynical fashion. With his Regency soul he had believed that women should be decorative, quite good at one or two things, but never so accomplished that they lost what he had called their essential appeal as women.

In all truth she had never driven her guardian's car on her own, but she had driven it with Marcus beside her at the wheel.

'Marcus was hardly the sort of man to allow his superb Rolls to be used by a woman,' she said, and hoped that her voice was convincingly casual. 'Now and again he promised me a car of my own, but it never came to that – as you once told me, *señor*, destiny weaves the pattern of our lives and it wasn't to be that my guardian should give me my own means of transport when I had my next birthday. The poor darling—'

She broke off, biting her lip, and hoped that mention of Marcus had detracted the Don from pursuance of whether or not she could drive. His frown flickered and he rose to his feet, his teeth clenched around his cigar. 'I have some letters to write.' He spoke abruptly and strode to the door of the *salita*, pausing there to look at her. 'Very well, remain here at the hacienda if it will suit you better – perhaps you wouldn't care to pretend in front of my friends that you are a radiantly happy bride. I shall give Juan Feliz instructions to drive you into town whenever you wish, but no hanky-panky, *querida*. Do you hear me?'

'Yes, *señor*,' she said demurely, but she didn't entirely relax until the door had closed behind his tall figure, clad in one of those dark velvet smoking-jackets which he sometimes wore in the evenings. As silence prevailed in the *salita* and all that lingered was his cigar smoke and the echo of his words, Persepha sank back against the tapestry of the sofa and folded her arms around a cushion, as if to shield herself from his possible fury when he discovered that she had lied to him.

He could be so utterly a devil when she, or anyone else, really angered him, but she knew that while he was absent from home she wouldn't be able to resist the temptation to take the car when the chauffeur's back was turned. He wouldn't punish Juan Feliz for something that she did – he wasn't that unjust, for his driver had a family of small children whom the Don found amusing in his spare moments.

If she could snatch a little freedom for herself, then the punishment that followed would be bearable. It was the feeling he gave her of always being watchful that made her need this freedom from him. She needed to talk with bantering ease to Gil Howard again, and not be on edge all the time as she was with her husband.

Husband ... it was a word that should mean companionship, security, and a warmth beyond the passion of the body. Don Diablo owned her, but when he flew off to the Argentine she would be her own mistress for seven heavenly days. She smiled at the prospect and couldn't wait for the day of his departure to come.

The Don left abruptly one morning, striding into her bedroom to wish her *adios*.

He leaned over her as she lay against the pillows, her hair shining against the lilac silk, and his arms imprisoned her slim figure beneath the silk sheets.

'Dare I hope that you might miss me?' he murmured, looking deep into her drowsy hazel eyes, as vital and spruce himself as if he had not spent half the night working with some of his men to save a foal that had blundered down a crevice. Persepha had been there as well, and she had wept after they had released the young horse and it had limped off to join its mother. She tried not to think of those tears as she gazed back at the Don, tiny nerves tightening like little bowstrings in her body as he trailed his fingers down the side of her neck.

'*Por deus,* but you're beautiful,' he said, the words rough and low in his throat. 'You can't know what you look like as you lie there, with your eyes the colour of dark honey as your pupils fill them up. I could break you in my hands, *queridisma,* and I shall if you ever betray me and give even a glance to another man. You are mine, my little iceberg, and I don't want to leave you here alone. Come with me! Put on a dress and fly with me to the Argentine. You will like it, I know.'

'No—' She turned away, pressing her face into the pillow, and unwittingly pressing his hand to her heart. 'Give me time – a little more time before I meet your friends. I – I can't pretend to be radiantly in love with you – you said so yourself.'

A tense silence followed her outburst, and then he forced her to face him, turning her over and holding her with hands that were no longer caressive.

'Then at least kiss me good-bye – and kiss me properly!'

'Very well,' she lay passive as his lips came down on her, and then as if her cool compliance woke the devil in him, his kiss became cruel, demanding, leaving her mouth feeling bruised. His eyes raked over her, as if he memorized every detail of her person before leaving her. His fingers took hold of a strand of her hair and as he drew it across his lips, she had a vision of him last night, forcing that foal to obedience, and safety. His lips came to bury themselves in the soft bareness of her shoulder and she clenched a handful of the silk sheet and strove for an icy stillness in his arms.

He let go of her and rose from the bedside, straightening the dark maroon tie that he wore with a lighter hue of maroon shirt, contrasting with the pearl-grey of his suit. He thrust a hand over his black hair, and his lips thinned into a stern line.

'We say *adios* but not good-bye, Persepha, no matter how much you want it. Wish me a safe flight, at least.'

Flight . . . the word seemed to fork through her. If only she might find a way to fly out of his reach when he was all those miles away.

'Are you wishing, instead, that the plane will crash?' he drawled, and before she could speak, even protest, he swung on his heel and strode to the door. 'There is an old saying, *querida*, that the devil looks after his own, so I shouldn't be too hopeful of being a fair young widow.'

With these words he was gone, and Persepha lay staring at the closed door, still seeing him in all his vital darkness, still hearing him as he spoke those sardonic words. All at once a shudder ran all through her and she flung back the bedcovers and ran to the door. She couldn't let him go believing a thing so cruel, not after last night, when she had seen the sweat plaster his shirt to his back as he fought to save a young animal from pain and fear. Whatever his attitude with regard to her, he had a strange compassion that she couldn't ignore.

'*Señor—*' But the gallery was empty and her cry echoed in the stillness, broken as a car started in the drive and sped off under the hacienda gateway, leaving her as she had wished, her own mistress.

She glanced around her bedroom and for the first time in weeks it was unoccupied by his presence at breakfast, and it had a curious emptiness that troubled her as she walked into the bathroom and stared at herself in the huge wall-mirror. Because of the slim, fair-haired figure that she saw reflected in the mirror she was here at the Hacienda Ruy, coerced into a loveless marriage through the sheer necessity of needing a home. That was what he liked, the Don her husband. That slenderness, that slim and youthful grace. Had she not pleased his dark eyes, then he would have left Stonehill without a backward glance, and when she stepped under the shower Persepha turned the shower nozzle so hard that the water pounded against her body, as if to wash from her skin his lingering touch. She didn't want to feel anything ... she wanted to be ice and marble where the Don was concerned.

She was in her bedroom and about to slip into her clothes when the door opened, as usual without a preliminary knock, and gave entrance to Carmenteira. The old woman carried a vase of white camellias for the white cane table that stood between the long windows, but Persepha knew that the flowers were just an excuse, a means by which the inquisitive old person gained access to the privacy of Persepha's bedroom, for the Don did not insist that his wife have a maid to wait on her. He allowed her to be reserved with everyone but himself.

'You are going to be lonely for a while, *señora.*' Carmenteira chuckled to herself as she fiddled with the flowers, sniffing at them and rearranging them with her stiff old fingers. 'But knowing the *padrone* as I do he would have left you with memories to last two weeks, let alone one. I would have thought that you'd have gone with him on his journey ... are you not afraid, *señora,* that in South America he will see a lovely Latin girl and find solace for his loneliness in her arms? Men will be men, when all is said and done, and the Don Diablo is much of a man, eh?'

Persepha gave the old woman a look of hauteur, for she thoroughly disliked these insinuating conversations, and the sly glances which were cast in the direction of the big bed with its rumpled pillows.

'It makes a break for a husband and wife to be apart now and again,' she said, and she had to suffer the scrutiny of this woman who had been so long at the hacienda that she was no longer treated as a servant but as almost a member of the family. The deep-set eyes stared at the garment which Persepha had just put on, a pair of cabin-boy breeches laced below the knee, in cat-green corduroy. She sniffed as Persepha put on a white cuffed shirt with the breeches.

'Boy's clothes,' she said. 'What's the matter with you, *señora*? Don't you like being a woman and need to wear those things in order to give yourself confidence? The Latin woman is born confident, for she knows her destiny from the cradle, and that is to be the centre and the joy of a man's life. But you – you rebel against your destiny.'

'My destiny?' Persepha looked scornful. 'I'd never have seen this place if it hadn't been for my father, and he left my mother even before I was born! I think that love means different things to men and women. I see only sacrifice in it for women; it's men who get out of it exactly what they want. Well, no man, not even your *señor hidalgo,* is going to make a slavish fool out of me, seeing only gloom when he isn't around, and basking like a cat in the sun whenever he shows his face. I'm my own person!'

'You are a little fool,' Carmenteira said. 'If you think that, then you don't deserve the honour of being mistress of this magnificent hacienda, which puts into the shade most other residences in Mexico. You are a shallow and ungrateful young woman, and the Don will realize his folly in marrying the likes of you, once he gets over his admiration for that silky white skin of yours and those honey-coloured eyes, not to mention the white-gold hair. You've taken his eye, my lady, but you haven't taken his heart, have you?'

'How dare you be so insolent!' Persepha could actually feel herself trembling at her resentment of her life here, among people who neither understood her nor gave her any sympathy. Tears rose up in her throat and threatened to turn her into a weeping fool in front of this mocking old woman.

'Get out!' Her voice was thick, her eyes blurred, as she flung out a hand towards the door. 'Go on, get out of my room and stay out of it! I – I've just about had enough of your insinuations – you think everyone's afraid of you because they take you for a witch who can cast spells. I only take you for what you are, a grubby old woman with nothing better to do with your time than to make mischief with it, and you just couldn't wait for the Don to turn his back before you came in here with your nasty remarks. I know you resent me, you and the rest of the household – know you compare me to the mistress you might have had – well, she's dead and I'm alive, and I'm not going to tolerate any more the way you come in here without even the decency of knocking on the door. I'm English and we like a bit of privacy, do you hear me? You'll stay out of my room from now on and you'll keep your opinions to yourself – for as you pointed out, Carmenteira, I am the mistress of the Hacienda Ruy, and as such I don't have to take rudeness from you or any other member of the staff. Is that understood?'

All through this outburst Carmenteira had looked at Persepha with eyes that gleamed like pieces of jet buried in parchment, but curiously enough the look was not vindictive.

'So,' she said, 'the *Inglesa* has some fire in her after all, and she is not entirely the milk-and-honey creature that she looks. All the same, *señora,* would you deprive a poor old creature who has worked hard for this family of the privilege of speaking her mind? Are you afraid of the truth when you hear it?'

'Not afraid,' Persepha walked to the door and held it open, 'just human enough to resent comparison to the Latin paragon you might have had here in my place. No doubt she would have welcomed you in her bedroom, and you could have shared all sorts of secrets and all sorts of hopes regarding the future sons and daughters of the house. I'm sorry I can't oblige on that score, but I am English and nothing on earth is ever going to change me into a Latin woman – even your incantations!'

Carmenteira came to the door and stood there looking at Persepha, whose eyes were sparkling both with temper and tears. 'It's very true,' she said. 'You will never be like a Spanish woman, for you will never want to give the Don a generous parcel of children. Be that as it may, he will want a son of you for his trouble in going to England to get you. As you say he learned of you from the peddler of pots and pans who came to stay here—'

'My father.' Persepha said it with a quiet dignity. 'Tell me before you go, is he buried on the estate? I've wondered about that, and all at once I feel like putting flowers on his grave. I never knew him, but he loved my mother in his own fashion, I understand.'

'There is a burial ground at the back of the chapel,' said Carmenteira. 'There I shall go when my time comes, for even you, *señora,* would not credit how old I am. I knew the *hidalgo*'s grandmother as a girl, and I held her hand when she passed from this life. But you won't hold mine, will you?'

At these rather pathetic words Persepha bit her lip, for she wasn't a hard person and it gave her no pleasure to quarrel with people. 'I am sure you'll live to be a hundred,' she said. 'Tell me, has the *hidalgo* no brothers or sisters? He never mentions them if they exist.'

'He had a young brother, *señora*, who died of polio some years ago. A fine young man named Alvarado, some years younger than the Don himself.'

At this surprising piece of information Persepha caught her breath and thought of what the Don had said about being instrumental in cleaning up the beach where they had gone only last week. He had said that polio had struck the region a few years ago, and it came as a shock to learn that he had lost his brother to that dread disease.

'What a shame,' she murmured. 'He has never mentioned that he once had a brother.'

'Perhaps the *señora* has never thought to ask him about those who have been close to him.' Carmenteira made her way out of the room, looking exactly like an old *bruja* in her long black dress, her skimpy hair black-netted, and around her neck an assortment of coins and charms. 'Take warning and appeal to the human side of him, young woman, or he may become the devil you take him for. In the men of Ezreldo Ruy there runs a streak of cruelty inherited from the past, but clever women know how to turn cruelty into kindness—'

'Kind?' Persepha gave a husky laugh. 'When the moon turns blue then will I believe in miracles!'

A little later, looking cool and fresh and just a little pink around the eyelids, Persepha walked through the patios and court gardens of the hacienda until she came to the tawny-walled little chapel that stood in a glade of lovely old trees with huge purple leaves like velvet, with close to its walls bushes of fuchsia and clumps of columbine and amaryllis. Also, almost up to one of the stained-glass windows, was a rambling branch of passion-flower, whose fruits were called the *maracuja*; the hammer and nails of the passion of Christ.

Persepha entered the chapel and found it cool and shady, with a polished aisle to the altar and the blue-robed figure of the Madonna on her dais. She walked slowly to the dais, and saw the flickering flames of candles burning just below the bare feet of Our Lady. The smoke mingled with the scent of flowers, and a sort of peace seemed to wind itself around Persepha's heart as she knelt and closed her eyes, which still felt a little heavy from those tears which wouldn't be held back after Carmenteira had left her.

Tears for herself, and for Marcus, and perhaps for the young man who had been named Alvarado. Sadness and confusion all mixed together, which being here in the chapel helped to assuage if not to cure. Persepha remained in that peaceful atmosphere for about fifteen minutes, and then she made her way to the burial ground, carrying the white camellias which Carmenteira had brought to her bedroom. She walked among the quiet headstones, some with angels carved upon them, and some with doves, and at last she found the plain headstone marked with the name that struck at her heart.

Charles Lennox Paget, departed from earth to heaven at the age of forty-four.

She knelt on the grass verge and laid the camellias on the grave, and up there in the ilex trees and birds sang as if they didn't know about heartache and the sorrows of love and hate.

Here far from the England where he had been born rested the remains of the man she had hardly ever thought about, for he had seemed dead to her long ago, and it was to Marcus that she had given her love and devotion. How strange that after all these years she should be here beside the father she had never known ... he and Marcus between them had shaped her destiny. One had aroused the

Don's curiosity about her, and Marcus had placed her in the Don's keeping in circumstances she had been unable to fight.

The treacherous tears sprang again to her eyes, and with a little touch of self-anger she swiftly brushed them away, and taking a single camellia from the bunch she went looking for one other grave in this private garden of memory, that of the young brother-in-law she was never to know, who had been named after an Aztec war-god, even as her husband had been named after the Devil.

When she left the quietness of the graveyard, where only the birds had movement and sound, she wandered on an exploration of the grounds that could not be interrupted by the abrupt appearance of Don Diablo. In the fig and mulberry orchards there was a low and sultry thunder of many bees busily at work among the blossoms of the fruit trees. She breathed the pungent air and felt an idolatry of the senses, a feeling of passionate warmth in the air that made her wince for those who were dead and cold and couldn't see the sun shining on petals and tiles and the shell-shaped basins of a lovely old fountain whose cascades of water were hued like the flashes of colour in lovely jewels.

She wandered from courtyard to patio, along paved walks where the flowers and shrubs were assisted in their growth by *ramblas* of water that sparkled in the sunlight. Butterflies hovered on wings that seemed made of crystal, and there were hanging cypress trees that made a veil of green, shading a tiled bench warmed by the sun, where Persepha at last relaxed with her thoughts.

It was no use denying that the hacienda was a sublime place, worked at by brown hands skilful and loving, until it was that perfect achievement where not a tree or a plant or a piece of stonework jarred on the eye or the senses. It created a deep response in anyone conscious of true beauty, similar to that induced by a haunting melody or a perfect piece of prose.

Persepha looked about her and wondered that she was the mistress of such a place. For the first time since coming here the realization struck her that she was the *padrona*, and she was stunned, and could understand at last why Marcus had been willing for her to become the wife of Don Diablo Ezreldo Ruy. Being the man he was, one who had taught her that love brought heartache, he would have gambled that she'd give her love to the hacienda itself and endure the husband who owned the estate.

Those had been the black and white terms by which Marcus had lived his life ... a throw of the cards ... a toss of the dice, and if a lucky number came up you took advantage of it. Added to which he had known that he was likely to die of a heart attack and that his property was entailed ... he hadn't known that he had been tossing not with the dice but with her heart.

Persepha sighed and reached for a tendril of green, unconsciously drawing it across her lips as the Don had drawn a strand of her golden hair.

In the next few days Persepha took the trouble to become acquainted with her beautiful home. It wasn't until the middle of the week that she asked Juan Feliz to drive her into town. She had decided, after all, not to risk the Don's displeasure by taking the car and causing damage with her uncertain driving. These few days on her own had taught her that it was a responsibility not to be ignored, being the mistress of so vast an estate, with so many people employed upon it, their livelihood, their welfare and in part their happiness, in the hands of the Don and whoever was closest to him.

That she was this person struck home forcibly to Persepha on the morning she heard shrill screams coming from the direction of the kitchen. She hastened from the *salita* and when she entered the big kitchen, with its tiled walls and immense cooking range, she was appalled to see two of the Mexican girls biting and clawing each other, their long black hair tangled around their passionate faces, the air alive with Spanish imprecations.

Another of the servants informed Persepha that the girls were fighting over a young man, a Lothario who had become entangled with both of them. She watched the scene for about a minute and when it became obvious that the girls were in no mood to listen to reason, she marched to the sink where she filled a jug with cold water and deliberately flung the contents over the furious pair.

At once their cries of anger became gasps of shock, and they stood there gaping at their mistress, fury quenched and water running down their faces.

'I will not have such behaviour in this house.' Persepha spoke in Spanish with slow deliberation, determined to make herself understood. 'You wouldn't behave so if the Don were at home, and you think that you can do as you please because I am here alone. I warn both of you, if you turn this kitchen into a cat-yard one more time, then I shall dismiss the pair of you.'

One of the girls then began to cry, but the other one tossed her wet hair and muttered that next time Loreta made eyes at her *amigo*, then she would use a knife on her and that would certainly be quieter.

'Don't be so foolish, Pilar. If the young man is so fickle, then you'd be wiser to find yourself another *amigo*. It's disgraceful, fighting like this over a man.'

'Wouldn't you fight, *señora*,' Pilar shot back at Persepha, 'if your man was enticed away from you by another woman?'

'I'd hope to have a bit more pride—'

'Pride?' Pilar scoffed. 'What has that to do with loving someone?'

'A woman has to have pride,' Persepha rejoined, 'or she has nothing.'

'I'd sooner have the love – the passion, *señora*.' The Mexican girl broke into a smile, flashing her vivid white teeth. 'You are not one of us, so you don't really understand. We take what we want, we fight for it, and then make sure that we keep it. Let Loreta glance once more at my *amigo* and I shall have her eyes for the breakfast of my mother's rooster!'

At this the girl Loreta gave a louder sob and dashed past Persepha from the kitchen. The girl called Pilar pushed the wet black hair from her brow, and her stance was a triumphant one, there on her bare brown feet. She had fought for what she wanted and Persepha couldn't help feeling a tingle of admiration for the pagan young creature.

'No more fighting,' she reproved. 'I won't allow that.'

She turned to leave the kitchen and saw the other servants looking at her with curious respect. She had dealt out a form of justice they could understand, and she knew they liked her for it.

Having, however, faced up to this small crisis, she just had to shrug off the weight of being *padrona* for a few hours, hopefully in the lighthearted company of Gil Howard. After telling Juan Feliz to get the car out, she went to her room and dressed with care, putting on a turquoise angora dress that reached to her knees, companioned by a pink angora cloche hat. Around her neck she hung the pearls which had belonged to her mother, and to the small lobes of her ears she attached the studs that matched the pearls. To her lips she applied a

116

tone of pink lipstick just a shade darker than her hat.

When her toilette was completed she looked very slim and chic – perhaps a little too eye-catching for a shopping expedition. If old Carmenteira happened to be pottering about in the hall she would be bound to wonder why her mistress was all dressed up, and Persepha knew very well that the old lady's allegiance to the Don made her a dangerous person to try and fool.

Persepha drew on her pink gloves and set her chin at a defiant angle. She wanted to go to town and wasn't going to be put off by the possible suspicions of Carmenteira. The old woman could only make surmises, and the household was well acquainted with her mysterious remarks and predictions of doom.

Assuming a casual air Persepha made her way down the curving staircase, but nerves tightened in her midriff when she caught sight of the bent figure, flicking with a feather duster at plant-pots and ornaments, making pretence to occupy herself so that she could take a good look at the mistress on her way to town.

'I see that the trousers have been discarded, *señora*.' The knowing eyes gleamed amid their wrinkles. 'You look so elegant that you might be on your way to a party – with a friend.'

'I have the *señor's* position to think of,' Persepha strove to retain her composure. 'It wouldn't be right for me to be seen in town looking anything but the perfect wife of a powerful landowner, would it?'

'Elegance and perfection are two different things,' said Carmenteira, her eyes narrowing as they ran over Persepha. 'The body can usually be dressed to look immaculate, but the intentions of the mind are too concealed for any woman but a nun to feel less than guilty about her thoughts and inclinations.'

'Guilty?' Persepha took her up, though it would have been wiser to continue on her way with her nose in the air. 'Why on earth should I feel anything of the sort?'

'You know that better than I, *señora*. I studied your tea-leaves this morning and I saw there an accusing finger and a display of fireworks. It could be significant, eh?'

'More likely a lot of nonsense.' Persepha knew that the old woman was only making guesses about where she was going, and playing on her nerves, and she smiled as she smoothed her pink gloves and made for the arched doorway that led out to where the car was parked, with Juan Feliz in his fawn-coloured uniform and peaked cap, looking very smart as he opened the car door for her.

'When we get to town,' she said to him, 'you can park in the square while I do my shopping. We have a nice afternoon for a drive, Juan.'

'*Si, señora.*' The chauffeur smiled politely, but in his eyes also there seemed to be a speculative glint, and as Persepha settled back in her seat she reflected that these people would watch her like hawks even without orders from the Don. His honour was their honour, and it might have been more diplomatic if she had worn a casual trouser-suit, for it was obvious that they didn't associate a woman in trousers with a flirtation.

Even as the word entered her mind it jarred on her ... but she had no intention of flirting with Gil Howard. She just wanted to talk lightly and easily about irrelevant matters, and to maybe hint that she might want to get out of Mexico and perhaps he could help in the matter of transport.

It was this latter thought that made the drive quite enjoyable for her; she felt that she was no longer quite on her own in an alien country among people who wouldn't understand or condone a wife's need to get away from her husband. Love? They'd snap their fingers at the idea.

It was her duty to stand by the vows she had made in church; they were holy and unbreakable.

But she wouldn't think about it right now. She would put it out of her mind and let her thoughts dwell on the pleasant prospect of seeing the grey-eyed American again, with his warm drawl and his open face that wasn't a dark mask concealing all sorts of secrets.

An hour later the car swept through the Mexican village on the outskirts of the town, and Persepha took her compact from her bag and made sure her face was cool and quiet, and that it didn't show in her eyes that she was a woman pursued by deeply unhappy thoughts. They drove into the town square with its equestrian statue, which she knew was that of an Ezreldo Ruy, for only they had such chiselled faces and such an air of command.

'How long will the *señora* be?' asked Juan Feliz as he assisted her from the car. 'Would the *señora* like me to come and carry her parcels?'

'I shall be about an hour,' she said, giving him what she hoped was a carefree smile. 'There's no need for you to tag along, Juan. I shan't be buying so very much, and just wanted an outing, really. You might as well find a café and have a refreshing drink – let's see, the time is now three o'clock, so I shall be back at the car around four o'clock. Don't worry about me. I'm not going to run away and get you into trouble.'

'Run away?' he said, instantly on the alert. 'The *señora* must not do that at any cost—'

'It's all right, Juan,' she assured him. 'I wouldn't want to get you into hot water with the *señor*, for I know what a temper he has. I'm just going to stroll around the shops, and I give you my oath I shall be back at the car by four. *Adios.*'

She walked quickly away from the chauffeur, but knew he was staring after her. She prayed that he wouldn't

119

follow her, and when she dared at last to glance over her shoulder she saw with relief that he had decided to trust her and was not tailing her. Thank goodness! She couldn't possibly have walked in on Gil Howard with the Don's driver at her heels.

When she arrived at the jewellery store she had a sudden attack of shyness and decided that she had better look in the window and select some article in which to have an apparent interest, just in case she was approached by one of the other assistants and couldn't bring herself to ask boldly for Mr. Howard to serve her.

She was standing there, gazing without any deep interest at a small jade clock that would look rather pretty on the desk of her boudoir, when she felt a tingling of her nerves that told her she was being scrutinized by someone. A little angrily she swung round, thinking the observer was Juan Feliz; that he had decided after all to keep a watchful eye on her.

'Look, I don't need a watchdog—' And there the words petered out, for it wasn't the uniformed figure of the chauffeur who stood there, a charming and quizzical smile on his face. It was Gil Howard, looking fit and sun-tanned and very grey-eyed, clad in a cream denim jacket, brown slacks, and a light brown button-down shirt open at his tanned throat.

'I thought a vision had come into town,' he drawled. 'I saw you pass by the sports shop along there, where I was looking at some tennis-rackets, and I just had to follow and make sure it was Persephone. This is my afternoon off, by the way, and we'd have missed each other if I hadn't spotted you in that most fetching outfit.'

'I – I came to town to buy a clock,' she said, pleased to see him and yet ruffled that he should so quickly presume that she had come on purpose to see him. 'This jade one – I'm going in now to have a closer look at it.'

'I really shouldn't waste your cash,' he said, looking amused. 'It's imported Hong Kong jade, and not really first-class stuff. I'm sure your husband has far more precious clocks at that hacienda of his – and where is he, Persephone? Where's the dark lord of Hades?'

'You shouldn't talk about him in that way,' she protested mildly.

'Will he have my skin for his saddle-bag?' Gil asked dryly. 'Is he conducting another business deal while you wander alone in the market place, looking more lovely than any woman has the right to look?'

When Gil Howard called her lovely she saw his eyes darken and she knew instantly that it rested with her whether she allowed this meeting to progress, or whether she terminated it before there was any real danger of it becoming a real flirtation. He was very attractive, and he was kind, and Persepha was in the vulnerable position of a wife very much possessed but not loved ... and she couldn't help but feel a stirring in her soul for someone to love her a little.

She sensed the danger ... it brushed against her, almost like the palpable wing of a moth. And then, as Gil smiled coaxingly, she brushed off the trembling wing, and let her own lips curve into a smile.

'My husband is conducting a business deal,' she admitted. 'In South America.'

'Wow, that's a nice long way for him to be! And so you decided to take advantage of his absence and came into town – to buy a clock?'

Her smile deepened, revealing a tiny dimple in her left cheek. 'If you feel I'd be wasting my money, Mr. Howard, then I'll forget about the clock.'

'I should, honey, and do call me Gil, for the mister sounds so formal between two people who are both free for the afternoon, who speak the same language, and who obviously like each other.'

'You take a lot for granted,' she reproved him, the dimple slipping out of sight again. 'I don't deny that I'm pleased to see you, but I'd better make it clear that I'm not a lonely wife on the prowl for a little solace. I did hope we could talk together again, in a friendly way—'

'I understand, Persephone, so don't go all tense on me.' His smile became warm and indulgent. 'Believe me, I wouldn't want anything to spoil this meeting, for I know you aren't a wife who goes out searching for kicks when her husband's back is turned. I've only to look at you to see you're a lady – a real one and not the kind who's stale candy wrapped up in sugar-floss. Look, I know a place where we can have a pot of tea and a plate of buttered scones? How does that grab you?'

'Oh, right here.' She pressed a hand to her midriff. 'Where is this dream place?'

He hesitated a moment, and then came a step nearer and looked down at her with frank grey eyes. 'My apartment, honey. It's only a few steps from here, and I promise you'll be as safe as a kitten in a cat's mouth with me. I won't eat you.'

It was Persepha's turn to hesitate, and to feel again that warning tremor, almost as if the ground moved beneath her feet. It was so palpable that she actually caught at Gil's sleeve. 'I – I could do with a cup of tea,' she said. 'And I think I trust you.'

'Then let that be enough,' he smiled. 'Shall we go?'

'All right,' she said, and as she fell into step beside him, the ground faintly quivered again, and Persepha silently called herself a weak-kneed little fool. The Don was miles away and he'd never know that she had snatched an hour to be with another man.

CHAPTER SEVEN

GIL's apartment was on the ground floor of one of those Latin houses with a circular courtyard and rooms leading from it. High cool rooms with louvred shutters and colour-washed walls, against which he had hung red and green gourds, a guitar with scarlet ribbons, and some quaint pots of plants that trailed their leaves down the walls.

He invited Persepha to take a seat on the couch, over which was slung a gaily fringed silk shawl, with big tapestry cushions at either end. In front of it stood a low table, with his American cigarettes in a box beside a lighter in the form of a silver owl. Across the floor lay a tufted rug in a variety of bright colours.

'This is a nice room,' said Persepha, looking around her with a smile from which the nervousness had vanished, which was partly due to the fact that it had taken them no more than a few minutes to reach the house, and she was convinced that she had not been seen by Juan Feliz. Now she could relax, and she did so against the silk shawl, and caught Gil's eyes studying her slender figure in the turquoise dress, whose soft bloomy material gave her a very vulnerable look. His eyes slid to her small arched feet in pink suede shoes.

'You should be nervous,' he said quietly. 'I've got to admit that if I had a wife like you, I'd be an angry man if you took tea with another guy.'

'Don't spoil things by paying me compliments,' she pleaded. 'It's the clothes – fine feathers always make fine birds.'

'You'd look fine to me in a piece of sacking,' he rejoined. 'Now how do you like your tea, with milk or lemon?'

'With milk, please. Shall I make it?'

'No, you sit there and make this place look pretty. Besides, I know where everything is, and my kitchen is always in a bit of a muddle, being rather on the small side. However, this apartment is close to the *avenida* and it has that courtyard attached, added to which the landlady isn't a bad sort and she doesn't come snooping around when a guy has a visitor.'

As he went into the kitchen, which adjoined his living-room, Persepha smiled to herself. By visitors he probably meant girls, for he was good-looking and virile, and he obviously liked female company. She let out her breath in a little relaxed sigh and heard him moving about in the kitchen, clattering spoons against china, and whistling softly and tunelessly to himself. It surprised her that he was divorced. She would have thought that any girl who was lucky enough to get him would have hung on tight to him, not gone looking for someone else when he was away working at such a dangerous job as diving for a sea-oil company.

'Do you have many visitors?' Persepha called out to him, her gaze upon the guitar with the scarlet ribbons, the sort that Latin girls were adept at playing, making that evocative music that somehow played on the senses, especially on a moonlight night. Sometimes at the hacienda she caught the sound of guitar music, and she would lean on the balustrade of her balcony and listen as it stole through the silence of the night, holding a promise that seemed forever out of reach.

'I do have the occasional guest for a meal,' Gil replied, coming into the room with a tray on which stood a teapot, cups and saucers, and a plate of scones, butter and strawberry jam. He placed the tray on the couchside table, and then brought the bowl of cube sugar and the jug of milk.

'Will you be mother?' he asked, putting a big plump floor-cushion to the other side of the table, on which he sat, stretching out his legs.

Persepha gave a tiny uncontrollable shiver at his words, but masked the tremor by leaning forwards and picking up the teapot. 'This is nice,' she said. 'I could almost believe I was back in England, smelling tea and jam, and being in a room as cosy as this one.'

'I should imagine the rooms at the hacienda must be very beautiful, and filled with rare objects, eh?' Gil busied himself buttering a scone and applying a generous helping of jam. 'Don't they appeal to you? I should think a girl like you would get a lot of satisfaction out of the unusual and the rare?'

'I didn't, you know, marry Don Diablo for his money,' she said, and a slightly hurt look came into her eyes as she handed Gil his cup of tea. 'The hacienda is beautiful, but it's a prison to me.'

'Then how come you married him, Persepha? If you didn't love the guy, then there'd have to be a pretty strong reason. Help yourself to scone and jam. Strawberry has always been my favourite.'

'Mine too,' she agreed, but right now she was dry and she settled back with her cup of tea and realized that she was going to have to talk about her marriage; that it was a subject that couldn't be avoided. 'The Don came into my life at a time when I lost someone very dear to me. I had no home, nowhere to go, and I hadn't really been trained for any kind of a job. I let myself be persuaded that marriage was my only safeguard against a world which had suddenly become empty of affection and filled with problems I had never had to face or deal with before. My guardian had always been there to make life easy for me, to cushion me against the sharp edges, and somehow I had become so used to doing what pleased him that when I learned that it was his last wish that I marry the Don, then I – I drifted into it, rather like a sleepwalker not wanting to wake to reality.'

Her voice died away, and she wasn't fully aware of just how significant was her silence to a young man very much of the world.

'But he soon brought you back to reality, eh?' Gil leaned a little forward and his grey eyes were very serious, without a hint of a smile in them. 'So he really did snatch you from the fields of play, seeing how lovely you were, and wanting you as he might want a Dégas painting or a rare porcelain. Only he didn't put you on a pedestal . . . It was a marriage in every meaning of the word except that of love. He took possession of you, his real-life Persephone.'

'Yes.' She gave him a diffident smile. 'It sounds incredible, doesn't it, as if I had made it up? In this day and age there can't be many girls who allow themselves to be led up the aisle as I was. He even selected a Catholic church and we were married by a Latin priest. He has bound me with gold and letters of fire, so he'll never divorce me or let me go of his own free will.'

'Then you'd have to run away,' Gil said quietly. 'You'd have to flee across the border into the States and find sanctuary there. You can't go on living a life of hell with a man you don't love, having to give yourself to him at a click of his imperious fingers. It's immoral!'

Persepha hadn't quite seen it in those terms, and she was taken aback by Gil Howard's vehemence. She hadn't realized that there was a streak of Puritanism in many Americans, inherited from forebears who had sailed to the new world in ships blessed by the priests of their own stern church. That he had been divorced didn't alter the fact that he was shocked by the idea of a girl living with a man against her will.

The angry glint in his eyes worried Persepha ... she didn't want him to become personally involved in her problem; all she had hoped for was that he might know someone who could be well paid to drive her out of Mexico when the time came.

'It's turn of the century,' Gil muttered, 'that a guy should live as he does, in feudal splendour way out there in the high country, and I suppose he thought it safe to leave you as he has most of the local residents on his pay-roll, none of whom would risk their jobs or their necks in order to help you get away. Well, he never reckoned on me, did he? The guy he looked at me on that beach as if I were a sand lizard he'd like to squash with his foot. He's damned arrogant for a guy with Indian blood in him!'

Persepha stared at Gil and the way his lip curled.

'Did you know that?' he asked her.

'Of course.' She looked faintly bewildered. 'He told me himself.'

'Before you married him?' Gil sat there frowning at her, his fair brows drawn together in almost a scowl.

'No – after we came here to Mexico. I hadn't given it much thought, except to think that he had exceptionally well-marked bones and a nose that might have been chis-elled – what's the significance? It's the Spanish blood in him that makes him so possessive and ruthless in his atti-tude towards me. There are Indians on the estate and some of them are extremely gentle, with deep soft voices and a great love of children.'

'They're still Indians!' Gil said it explosively. 'My dear girl, you really are the most innocent thing I've ever en-countered, so it's no wonder that *hidalgo* could trap you into his kind of marriage. What a quiver in his bow, a lovely English bride with skin like milk and hair like a sunbeam. No wonder he's chief of his tribe – he's clever!'

Persepha drew back against the shawl covering of the couch on which she sat, and the cup and saucer suddenly trembled in her hand and she put them down on the table. Her face had gone rather white. 'Stop that, Gil! I don't like the way you're talking!'

'I don't mean to upset of frighten you, honey, but I'll certainly do all I can to help you get away from Don Devil – that's what you want, isn't it? You've realized that you can't go on living with him – it must be pure hell for a girl like you. I bet before he happened along you'd never even had a real boy-friend and gone through all the normal flirtations, not if you had an elderly guardian looking after you. They can be more strict than even a real father.'

'Marcus wasn't elderly,' she protested, 'but he did ensure that I was kept rather sheltered, and I so liked his company that I didn't want to flirt with rather silly young men. Marcus always wanted me to make what he called a good marriage—'

'A super marriage!' Gil scoffed. 'Money's great to have around, if there isn't someone else holding the purse strings, and along with them the whip hand. You've thought about getting away, of course?'

'I – I've thought about it,' she admitted. 'But there are complications—'

'Bound to be,' Gil broke in, 'but they're not insoluble, not if you don't want them to be. You don't feel any love for the guy! You couldn't! He's of a different race and creed, and he's years older than you. He's made of you what we call in the States a rich man's plaything! And gee, you're so beautiful!'

Gil leaned forward and caught hold of her hands,

looking at their pale slenderness and the valuable rings that weighed upon them. 'These are worth a devil of a lot and could be sold, you know that?'

'I – I couldn't sell the rings,' she said hastily. 'That would be stealing, somehow, for they're Ezreldo Ruy family property, engraved on the inside of the bands with Latin words. I do have something else, a brooch he gave me, which is not an heirloom. I had thought about selling that—'

'Yeah, I remember it! a gorgeous dragonfly which was pinned to your dress that first time we met!' Gil looked into her eyes. 'Was that how come you walked into the jewellery store? You were going to ask if we'd buy it?'

'I was going to say that I'd like it valued, just in case I needed the money.' Persepha bit her lip, and though her hands moved in Gil's she didn't try to pull them away. 'I have thought about leaving the Don, but he has my travel documents and my passport, and I can't go far without them, and if I couldn't get out of Mexico he'd be bound to find me, and it would be worse for me afterwards.'

'Worse?' Gil gripped her hands. 'What do you mean? He doesn't beat you, does he? That would be intolerable!'

'I mean he'd keep an even closer watch on me, for he's too subtle, Gil, to actually beat a woman. He doesn't need to use brute tactics.'

'You mean he can make you quail with a look, eh?'

'Something like that.' She pulled her gaze from Gil's and looked instead at the coloured gourds on the wall; they had a bright irrelevance about them that made her envious of Gil's freedom and his present carefree way of life. He probably made just enough at the shop to keep him in food, clothes and rent, and Persepha thought how cowardly she had been to distrust her own ability to find work and be independent. She had let the Don take control of her life, and now like a moth in a net she was struggling to get free, and terrified that he'd clip her wings before she got beyond his reach.

'Do you happen to know where your husband keeps your papers?' Gil asked. 'Surely you can get hold of them?'

'They're locked in his desk, and as you can imagine I daren't ask for them; right away he'd guess why I wanted them.'

'So he's under no delusions about the way you feel about him? He knows you hate him, but he's not letting go, huh? Well, it's typical of his kind; they don't credit women with any real human rights and want them for – well, I won't put it into words. I'll spare your blushes, Persepha, for you know well enough what I mean, don't you?'

She knew and didn't want to discuss that aspect with Gil Howard. It was far too personal and painful, and pulling free of his grip she rose to her feet and went to the archway that led out to the courtyard, the oval-shaped door thrown open to let the air and the fragrance of roses and carnations into the apartment. They grew in colourful profusion around an old fountain and over the circular walls, and Persepha thought again how fortunate Gil was to have this unpretentious and undemanding life.

'I do like this place,' she exclaimed. 'What about you, Gil? Do you enjoy living in Mexico?'

'Sure, it has its advantages, and here you can live a bit cheaper than in the States, for there's so much fruit around, and I'm crazy for buttered corn and chilli. The clothes are lightweight and inexpensive, and there's always the sea and the sunshine.'

'And the pretty Latin girls,' she smiled. 'Some of them are incredibly attractive, with that raven hair and those huge brown eyes.'

'Sure,' he drawled, 'but have you seen how they get when they're about thirty? A girl like you, honey,' and as he spoke he came and stood behind Persepha at the archway, 'you'll still be lovely when you're sixty, slim and fine-boned, with silvery hair.'

'Don't let's get sentimental, Gil,' she said lightly, though her body tensed from the touch that she felt was imminent. She couldn't ignore the fact that she had come willingly to Gil's apartment, and he could be forgiven for thinking that an unhappy wife was in need of consolation from a man a little kinder and more lighthearted than her husband. However, she was in enough of a pickle without getting emotionally involved with another man, and Gil Howard had to be held at arm's length.

'Have you a girl-friend, or two, here in Mexico?' she asked him. 'You don't strike me as the type who likes his own company.'

'A girl or two drifts in and out of my life,' he admitted. 'Since my break up with Lois I've been a little wary of getting deeply involved, for I really was fond of that kid. She was a singer in a Santa Monica club and she just wouldn't take to the travelling life with me. It's ironical that now I'm a bit more settled I no longer have a wife to share my home.'

'Poor Gil.' Persepha reached a hand to a vine that clung and scrambled around his doorway and her fingers fondled the mauve flowers that grew among the ferny green leaves. Land of a rampant sun and a rich flowering, and a rueful way of life ... for her. She might almost have grown fond of it, had she come here to Mexico of her own free will.

'And poor Persephone.' His hands closed over her slim shoulders. 'Was there a knight who came along to console her, who in every way looked and behaved differently from her dark lord?'

'I – don't know.' Persepha smiled a little, drew herself out of his hands and walked out to the courtyard, where the warmth had a sultriness she hadn't noticed before. She glanced up at the sky and instead of being a clear blue it had a saffron tinge to it, as if the sun had gone molten and some of the brazen gold had seeped into the sky.

'Are we in for a storm?' She turned in some alarm to Gil, for soon she had to leave and she had heard that when it rained in Mexico the heavens opened and the rain poured down mercilessly. Driving in such a deluge would be a nerve-racking experience, for part of the country on the way back to the hacienda was like a desert, scattered with strange clumps of cacti and outcrops of rock and sand. With the rain beating down hard it would be like driving into the sea itself.

Gil studied the sky and his fair brows drew together in a frown as he pulled at the neck of his brown shirt. 'Boy, it has grown murky, and I do recall one of the old guys in the market-place remarking that the earth was grumbling, which is their way of saying that rain is needed. If this country goes too long without rain, then the earth cracks open and great yawning mouths appear into which people have fallen.'

Persepha thought of the crevice into which that foal had fallen and she gave a shiver, one of inward coldness for her skin felt as warm as if she stood near a fire. 'Gil, I'd better be going,' she said. 'I have to be back at the car by four o'clock, otherwise the driver will become anxious. And if there's going to be a downpour, Juan Feliz and I should start the drive home before it comes flooding down. It won't be any fun for him driving in a deluge, and he'll be worried all the time about having me for a passenger.'

'You mean the Don would give him hell if anything

132

happened to you?' Gil took hold of her and swung her to face him, and there seemed to be a flicker of storm in his grey eyes as they studied her tense face. 'Are you sure the *hidalgo* isn't crazily in love with you? You're lovely enough to get under the toughest skin—'

'No – he doesn't love me, in the way you mean.' Persepha spoke with a conviction which even torture couldn't have shaken. She knew, as no one else did, that the Don had never spoken of love and had only ever shown that he possessed her. She knew, as Gil didn't, that her husband had given his heart to someone else – a woman into whose grave he had wanted to leap on the day they had buried her. 'Don Diablo merely owns me, and he has a possessive nature, and it would make him furious if his property was damaged in any way. I'm going now – I must. Thank you for tea, and for letting me talk about my problems. I don't imagine that you're often used as a psycho-analyst, but I'm very grateful to you – Gil, please let me go! I have to go!'

'I'll let you go, honey, if you promise you'll come again.' He drew her forward until her angora dress was brushing his shirt and slacks. 'In some ways you're as soft as a kitten and you need to be petted. I guess the Don takes you by the scruff of your neck and makes you claw and yowl. You need to be made to purr, Persepha, and I'm not too bad at getting girls into a sensuous mood.' And as he spoke Gil drew his hand down the side of her dress to her hip, caressingly. 'Wouldn't it be a nice way of getting back at him, to have someone to make you feel good? Someone like me?'

'Do you know,' she said quietly, 'what he'd do if he found out that I was making a cuckold of him, with any man?'

'But there's no reason on earth why he should find out.' Gil grinned down at her. 'You are a little innocent, you know. Look at us right now! Does anyone know that we're here together? You came to town during the siesta, and believe me when Mexican people take their siesta it takes the devil or an earthquake to wake them up. That's how we could arrange it—'

'No.' She spoke sharply. 'I don't care about the Don and his almighty honour, but I care about my own. You said yourself, Gil, that I'm not the sort for extra-marital antics, and you were right. I'd feel cheap and brazen, like some woman the Don and I saw the other day, so accustomed to giving herself that she almost does it in front of other people. Ugh, I'd sooner be dead!'

'Well, thanks,' he drawled. 'I had no idea that I struck you as being less attractive than a hole in the ground.'

'Oh, it isn't that! You are attractive, Gil, and I like you, but I don't want an affair – all I want is to be free.' She sighed, and then gave a frightened gasp as the very ground seemed to tilt beneath her feet, throwing her forward against Gil's chest. They clung, but not amorously, and then it came again, that curious and terrifying tremor, much harder this time, throwing the pair of them right off their feet to the hard courtyard stones.

'It's a quake!' yelled Gil, and Persepha just caught the words a second before her forehead struck a partly raised stone and sent her flying into a painful, stunning darkness.

When she came to herself, she wasn't lying on the ground but on the softness of a bed, and there was an icy coolness against her forehead, easing the ache that throbbed there. She gave a groan and saw tiny flashes in front of her eyes as she forced them open. Everything spun round and she couldn't focus her gaze for several moments, and then gradually she became aware that a lamp was on, throwing shadows against a pale wall and a white ceiling ...

one shadow was that of a man bending over her, and when she stirred and mumbled a name, he bent a little closer, and moved the ice-bag to her temple.

'Persepha, honey, are you all right? My, but you gave me an almighty scare, you were out so long!'

She stared at the face in the lamplight and let her hazy eyes wander over the rugged features, tanned but not dark; the eyes grey and not like deep wells of smouldering jet.

'Gil?' His name was a question, not a statement, as if she wasn't yet sure of him. 'W-where am I? W-what happened?'

'A hell of an earth tremor,' he told her. 'You hit your head and I brought you indoors – how do you feel, honey? It was quite a crack and it put you out for a couple of hours or more. I was thinking of dashing out for a doctor when you started to groan and move about. Does it hurt a lot?'

'Enough,' she managed weakly. She tried to sit up and again the room spun round and she collapsed against the pillow. 'M-my head aches and everything is going round, Gil. And it's dark!'

'Honey, the lamp is on.' A note of alarm came into his voice. 'You can see me, can't you? You can see?'

'Yes—' Her gaze stole round the room, taking in the pale walls, the chest of drawers, the fluttering shadows as the flame of the lamp moved back and forth. 'It's night time, Gil! It's night and I shouldn't be here!'

As she began to struggle to sit up, Gil firmly pressed her back against the pillow. 'You mustn't move just yet, honey. You could have a touch of concussion after that crack on the head, and I'd be doing you more harm than good if I allowed you to get out of bed. Now just relax and don't get into a panic. The quake has died away and now if you listen you'll hear the rain – hear it?'

She lay back reluctantly and glanced over towards the window, where the thin curtains couldn't muffle the sound of heavy, battering rain, like fingers of iron knocking on the glass and threatening to break it.

'The rain came and the heat lifted,' said Gil. 'Thank heaven it did, otherwise we might have had some really colossal tremors that would have caused real damage. It will rain heavily for hours, and then the courtyards will be overflowing with flowers – they'll be smothered in them. Great!'

'Oh yes,' she echoed, 'it's really great that I'm stranded here with you, with no hope of getting away for hours – ooh, my head! It feels as if I've been kicked by a mule.'

'That's better than being numb,' he told her, and circling an arm around her, so she was cradled, he applied the ice-bag to the nape of her neck. 'There, I bet that feels good, huh?'

'Mmmm,' she had to admit that it felt awfully good, and she only wished that her nerves could be so easily treated. 'I know it isn't any of your fault, Gil, but I'm worried about Juan Feliz, and what will the others at the hacienda be thinking?'

'I guess like sensible people they'll assume that you've been trapped somewhere by the heavy rain – that you're taking shelter. My sweet girl, there's no need to get so hot and bothered about it, for you'll only make yourself feel dizzier. Come on, you must relax. That husband of yours can't blame you for an act of nature; he can't say that the elements conspired to make it possible for you to spend the night with me, now can he?'

'The – night?' She gazed at Gil with such horrified eyes that he gave a rueful laugh.

'There you go again, Persepha, looking at me as if I'm some kind of a rake. Those two men in your life have taught you to be positively hostile towards younger men, and that isn't fair. I bet I'm a nicer fellow than either of them, or do you consider that a debatable point?' He quizzed her with a grin in which relief that she was all right was mingled with a sort of boyish triumph that she was marooned alone with him. Outside in the courtyard they could both hear the rain splashing down, a drowning deluge that looked like going on for hours, flooding over the old stones and gurgling in the roof gutters, and bringing into the room a jungly smell.

'I shouldn't want it to become a debatable point,' she said seriously. 'It does sound as if I'm going to have accept your hospitality, and the way my head feels I don't want to think about tomorrow and what kind of an excuse I'm going to have to make when I get home.'

'You can only tell the truth,' he said. 'You took shelter from the quake and the rain and had to stay the night with the – er – people who gave you shelter.'

'You see,' she took him up, 'the absolute truth is out of the question. I'm here with you alone, and how would that sound? I'm going to be asked the name, address and status of the people with whom I supposedly stayed overnight. I just know I am!'

'But your husband's in South America,' said Gil. 'He can't act the inquisitor directly you get home, and by the time he does arrive, your sense of guilt would have worn off and any white lie you tell him will have the casual ring of truth. You can just say the people were kind, and you were in too much of a spin from a blow on your head to think to ask their name, and all you really remember is that they lived in a house with a courtyard. There are dozens of such houses hereabouts, and if you play on his sympathy with regard to getting bumped on the head, there's no need for him to ever know the real truth.

'You're a woman, honey,' Gil's eyes slipped over her, 'and there's a bit of an actress in every female. Now, do

137

you reckon you could drink a tot of brandy? It will help steady you.'

'I – I think I'd prefer a cup of coffee,' she said, and though she was looking about her for her bag and her shoes, it did rather look as if she were avoiding his eyes, and he said gruffly:

'I don't plan to make you tipsy so I can seduce you. There's no fun in it for me if the gal's reluctant, and you're scared stiff of that husband of yours even finding out about me.'

She looked at him then, at his ruffled hair above his brow, and that slight boyish scowl that came and went was like a breeze through the trees compared to the Don's dark frown, and his fearless unconcern that a woman should want him or not.

Yes, looking at Gil Howard she could see that he liked to be thought well of by a woman and it would bother him to have to force a response from someone. Maybe it was that attitude which had broken up his marriage; he had not forced Lois to live his kind of life but with a free and easy shrug he had let her go her own way, and that way had led her straight into the arms of another man.

Persepha could feel a slight smile trembling on her lips . . . good-looking Gil was a trifle vain; he expected girls to fall for him and wasn't prepared to fight for their affection. Thank heaven, she thought, that he hadn't the disposition of a Don Diablo, otherwise this night would be fraught with peril.

'What are you smiling about?' Gil demanded.

'I'm smiling because you're so nice,' she said. 'If a girl has to spend a night with a man not her husband, then I'd vote for you any time. I really don't think of you as a satyr, and I just happen to fancy coffee more than brandy.'

138

'I see.' He looked quizzical as he sat on the side of the bed looking at her, her pale hair tousled and damp from the ice-bag, with a livid bruise against the left side of her forehead. The turquoise dress which had been so immaculate was dirtied from her fall and rumpled above her knees. There was a ladder in her sheer nylons, and a slight graze on the side of her chin.

'You look marvellous even when you've been through the wars,' he told her, 'so I'm not sure I should take it as a compliment that I'm not your idea of a dangerous guy. Are you saying that compared to Don Devil I'm a tame sort of fellow?'

'I believe,' she half-smiled, 'that half the men in the world would outshine my husband for gentleness. He has that quality which makes a Spaniard saunter into a bull-ring – the courage to be cruel. I don't think that Americans or Englishmen possess that type of almost fatalistic nerve, for I don't think they really believe in hell as the Latin does. He believes he's going to burn no matter what he does; he has a dark faith in original sin, far more so than the Anglo-Saxon.'

'Hence the Inquisitorial,' drawled Gil. 'Live hard here on earth, for there's no hope in heaven, ye sinners!'

'Something like that.' Her smile quivered and she put a hand to her aching brow. 'Poor Desdemona was choked to death because of a handkerchief, so heaven help me if the Don ever finds out that I spent a night in the apartment of a handsome American!'

'Glad, anyway, that I'm not altogether unattractive to you.' Gil leaned forward and gently touched her face with his hand. 'Poor kid, you must try and get away from the Don before he returns from his business trip. I'll help all I can – come with you, maybe.'

'It's getting hold of my passport and paper—' She bit her lip. 'I wonder if it can be managed—?'

'Sure, find a hammer and break the lock of his desk.'

'I mean – getting away from him. He has a long arm and owns so much of this territory, and probably a sizeable share of the railway. I sometimes think that if I got as far as England, he'd find me and drag me back to Mexico. He doesn't love me, but he chose to marry me, and that makes me part of the Ezreldo Ruy hierarchy. I – I no longer have a fate of my own. I am bound to him and his plans for the future.'

Persepha pressed her fingers to her forehead and had a vision of the Don's concern had she fallen to the court-yard stones in front of him – a concern entirely rooted in his desire for a son. By now she would have a physician looking her over to make sure her childbearing prospects weren't damaged – of that she was ironically sure. High wind or water wouldn't have stopped the Don from getting a doctor to her side.

She closed her eyes as a wave of dizziness swept over her, and she seemed to spin away from the lamplit bedroom of Gil's apartment into the silken realms of her suite at the hacienda ... she seemed to feel around her a hard bronzed arm, binding her close but never letting her into the heart that beat so firmly under the warm chest with its pelt of hair so dark against his skin. Like a tiger with its prey he held on to her even in his sleep, and she always lay so still unless he stirred, feeling the lift and fall of his muscular chest, the very beat of his heart in her bosom.

'Persepha?' A hand gently shook her shoulder. 'Honey, are you all right?'

At the touch, which was somehow unfamiliar, she gave a little moan of protest and her eyes fluttered open. 'I'm all right.' She stared up at Gil. 'Just tired—'

'I'll make that coffee, huh?'

'Yes — that would be nice.'

But she slept again before he returned, and the next

time she awoke the morning light was in the room and the rain had died away. The night was over and the day had dawned, and Persepha had to return to the Hacienda Ruy in a crumpled dress, in a hired car, to face the silent accusations of the Don's household, which would become voluble as soon as he came home from South America.

CHAPTER EIGHT

SHE was standing upon the high terrace when she caught her first glimpse of the silver car bringing the Don home to the hacienda. Her fingers clenched the balustrade for she didn't doubt that he would have asked a number of seemingly casual questions, and Juan Feliz would have answered them. The earth tremors of last week would have been mentioned; the Don would have been concerned that no damage had been done to the hacienda. It would have been one step from the brink for the chauffeur to then inform his master that on the day of the tremors he and the *señora* had gone to the shops and after that she had vanished, only to reappear hours afterwards at the hacienda, dishevelled and bruised.

The sun flickered like lightning on the framework of the car as it sped in beneath the great archway, where the big iron gates were thrown open, the escutcheon of the Ezreldo Ruy family wrought into the iron itself. The car came to a halt in the courtyard and the door opened at once, thrusting outwards to allow the long swing of his legs in dark fawn suiting. Persepha stared downwards at the familiar dark head, the lean and powerful body, the way his long shadow fell across the sunlit tiles as he stood there, looking around him, absorbing all that meant so much to him. Jade leaves against tawny-cream walls, ivory petals, the drift of a butterfly with flamy wings.

His house, set like a jewel in stone above the world, its foundations intermingled with those of an Aztec temple, just as his blood was intermingled with the old barbarities and the pagan beliefs.

And then, as if his quick blood sensed her presence, he

glanced up and his dark eyes caught and held her gaze. Not a muscle moved in his face; not a hint of a smile stirred in his eyes. He might have been looking at a stranger instead of his wife, and because she was afraid of him since that night with Gil Howard and couldn't act with the ease of other women, she just stood there like a pale statue and looked about as welcoming as a thing carved out of marble.

Then with a slight glint of irony coming into his eyes, the Don inclined his head to her, the sunlight playing across his scalp and bringing out the blue-black lights in his hair. It was like a plume, she thought, on the helmet of a *conquistadore*, and the tips of her fingers seemed to tingle as she remembered the feel of his hair, thick and crisp and never oiled.

He was home and once again he would come and go in her bedroom-suite, the bed-lamp throwing his shadow high up the wall as he came through the adjoining door, walking silent and supple across the vicuna rug, pulling the robe from his brown shoulders as he came, flinging it from him as he reached for her and pulled her free of the concealing covers.

Persepha waited on the terrace for him to come to her, knowing that like a dutiful wife she should go downstairs to greet him, but Carmenteira would be there, mockery incarnate in her eyes as she waited for Persepha to lie to him about that night of the earth tremors and the torrential rains.

'Old witch!' Persepha muttered, but there was no real intensity in her words. She didn't really dislike the old woman, for if she was possessive about the Don, and fiercely defensive about his honour, it was because she was Latin and had served this household from a very young girl. If he had to have the English girl to satisfy him, then the old woman understood, for he was *muy hombre*, as she was fond of saying. But she didn't have to approve his choice, and Persepha knew that she waited, like a black widow spider, for some flaring disagreement to throw them apart so that he would cease to even want her. Then like other *padrones* he would take a Latin mistress, and that – so Carmenteira thought – would put the nose of the English girl completely out of joint.

Carmenteira thought her proud, and in her estimation only men had the right to be proud and self-willed. She was old, of another time, and she believed that women should be humble and grateful for a man's attentions. She wanted to see Persepha humbled, one way or another, and that was why Persepha stayed up here and waited to greet the Don in privacy.

She steeled herself for that meeting, and had even dressed for it in an apricot-toned dress of spotted chiffon, with a deep frill at the hem and a softly detailed neckline. It suited her colouring, and the chignon style of her hair leaving her slim neck bare and vulnerable, with tiny gold tendrils of hair against her creamy skin. She had coloured her lips lightly, but wore no other cosmetic apart from a dab of perfume.

He had been away from her for ten days, and she hoped that if he had missed her, he might not be overly curious about that night she had spent away from the hacienda.

Her hand stole to her temple, from which the mark of her fall had ebbed away. It might have been a far worse blow had she not been wearing a hat, but the pink cloche had cushioned the side of her forehead against the full force of her head hitting the ground as the heaving of the earth had thrown her right out of Gil's arms. That upraised stone could have left her with a scar, and she didn't think that the Don liked his possessions damaged in any way; he would dislike a scarred woman as much as he

144

would a cracked wine goblet, for perfection pleased his eye and he had handled her much in the same way as she had seen him toy with a rare wine glass or a jade object from his collection in the *sala,* running his lean dark fingers over the silky surface and the slim contours, seeking to find only a sensuous pleasure.

Well, she wouldn't just stand here, like a child waiting to be punished, and fingers gripping the chiffon handkerchief that matched her dress she walked to one of the deep cane chairs and sat down, crossing her legs with an assumption of ease and admiring abstractedly the design of her ivory-coloured, high-heeled sandals.

Down in her midriff she could feel a riot of nerves and it was impossible to face with a calm mind the thought of having him close to her again . . . she recalled the moment of their parting and what she had said to him . . . and what he had said to her, about both of them getting their wish. Ten days, and his eyes would take in every inch of her, possessing her without even touching her.

She laid her head back against the lime-green cushion of the chair and closed her eyes against the sun . . . she would pretend to be dozing when he came to her, as if it troubled her in no way at all that he was home again.

For this moment, and the next, she was alone in the hot silence of the tropical noon, which dazed even the cicadas, and there stole to her nostrils the subtle perfume of the frangipani flowers that clambered all over a nearby wall, spreading from a tree planted years and years ago and now grown strong and high, making a small temple of its boughs and filling the nearby air with that mystic flavour.

Flower of temples, and flower of love . . . she gave a little shiver and wished that it had been possible to get away from Mexico before the Don's return. But there had been no way to get hold of her passport; she had gone to the door of his office one evening, intending to try his desk in the hope that he might have left it unlocked, but to her amazement, and her anger, she had found the door of his office firmly locked. He had guessed that she might try to find her travel papers and her passport, and so as an added precaution against her recovery of them, he had during his absence locked her out of his study. She had wanted to pummel at the door, scream and kick at it in her impotent sense of fury at being treated not only like a prisoner but as a child not to be trusted.

But I'm not to be trusted, she thought idly. *He knows I'll go, if I ever get hold of my papers! He knows I'll run away if I get the chance.*

Her hand flung out towards the frangipani of its own accord and her fingers crushed the tiny, star-like flowers with a cruelty she was unaware of; all she knew in this moment was a need to find ease for all her tumult of heart and body, and she was still too unworldly to realize that only by inflicting pain could one's own pain be eased.

It was her innermost nerves that felt his approach, for he had come through the open glass doors before she heard him. She tensed and forced her eyes to remain closed, until shadow fell across her eyelids and she knew him to be standing over her, tall against the sun. He didn't speak and she knew that he was waiting with diabolic patience for her to lose control of her apparent composure.

The silence stretched until it tore at her nerves and she couldn't stand any longer that silent, curious, mocking scrutiny. He knew she was wide awake and only pretending to doze in the sun. He knew it to be a battle of wills, and she could actually feel the magnetic power of his gaze penetrating into her mind ... her very bloodstream.

Without laying a finger upon her the Don made her

open her eyes to him, and he filled the world like a dark shadow, his eyes unfathomable because the sun was behind him.

Still he waited, and she knew that she had to speak first, had to say something, and because she had shown him that she was not deliriously overjoyed to see him again, she found it comparatively easy to murmur a casual, 'Hello, *señor*. You're looking well.'

He was looking as tanned and lean as a hard-riding Indian, yet she wondered if it was her imagination that seemed to see a deeper incisiveness to the lines beside his dark eyes. 'I trust that your business deal was brought to a satisfactory conclusion?' she added. 'Will you now make lots more money?'

She was inwardly pleased by her own flippancy, and then she flinched as he suddenly leaned down, gripped her wrists and pulled her to her feet, so swift an action that it seemed to check the beat of her heart as she was swung into the full play of the sun and studied so intently that she felt like some *objet d'art* which had a flaw he had to search for.

She flung up her chin and gave him a proudly defiant look. She had done nothing of which she need feel ashamed and she wasn't going to be forced to defend herself when she was an innocent victim of what Gil had called an act of nature.

'Well, Persepha, are you disappointed that the plane didn't crash and land me in hell instead of Latin America?' As he drawled the words he carried to his lips the hand whose fingers were drenched in the scent of the frangipani, and as he kissed her skin, running his lips along each separate finger, she saw his nostrils quiver and he suddenly brought her palm right against his face and he breathed that scent which her warm skin had intensified.

'Dare I hope that you missed me for even an hour?' His words moved his lips against her palm, and the sensation was curiously intimate, so that she wanted to snatch away her hand before a hot flood of sensuous memory flooded over her. Too late, for he gripped her around the waist and brought her so bone-close to him that only a shadow could have slithered between them.

When he walked, when he rode, whenever he entered a room he had that *élan vital* of a body in perfect control of its every muscle, but for a wild moment, a raking second or two, Persepha felt him quiver from his neck to his heels as he locked her against him, until he must have felt every particle of her slim body through the thin chiffon of her dress.

He moulded her to his hard frame as she knew he moulded her to his will, as if she were made of clay and could eventually be made to bend to his every whim and fancy, until she lost her own identity and became part of him.

'No!' She jerked her head aside and wouldn't succumb to that power he could assert over everyone; in her case a physical power with a wild thread of passion running in it, reaching out to those dark, secret places where love didn't warmly glimmer to make of passion a splendid thing.

'No – I can't kiss you!' She cried out the words as if they were a confession she was making on the rack. All he had to give her was passion, and she didn't want that . . . not that.

'And why can't you kiss me, Persepha?' He gripped her chin in his hard fingers and made her look at him, almost hurting her as he forced her to a full frontal scrutiny. His black eyes looked down into hers, a little flame smouldering at the centre of each one. 'Have you something on your conscience, my dear? Has something happened that

148

you feel ashamed of? Come, why not tell me, make a clean breast of it? What have you done, smashed some of my fine glassware, or spilled ink on the panel Persian rug in the dining *sala*?'

He was mocking her, being the cruelly smooth inquisitor leading up to the real accusation. Persepha hated him for that and her fingers clawed at his jacket, but couldn't reach to his face, for she was too tightly crushed to him, held as if in a vice that might break her bones.

'Y-you've been grilling Juan Feliz, haven't you?' she panted. 'You've found out about that – that night I had to spend in town, and you're wild as hell about something I just had no control over—'

'Ah, was it as impetuous and demanding as that, *mi vida*, that you could not control what occurred – that night?'

His face seemed devilish to her as his voice sank down on that final word. He frightened her more than he ever had, and she felt a kind of terror taking hold of her that he knew about Gil – yet how could he know? They had been so utterly careful about the hiring of the cab; Gil had telephoned from the store where he worked and the cab-driver had picked her up in the town square, where she had waited by the equestrian statue. No one had seen her ... and then her heart gave a little trip that made her catch her breath.

There had been someone hanging about ... in her relief at getting out of town she had quite forgotten until now that there had been a man in the square that morning. One of those intensely thin and sallow Mexicans, with a coal-dark moustache that drooped at the ends like a bandit's, and eyes like shotgun pebbles that bored into a woman. She had been so relieved by the arrival of the cab that she had quickly pulled open the door, her edge of panic making her voice rise as she had given the driver her address.

As these images flashed again through her mind she stared up at the Don her husband, and her heart warned her that he knew something . . . perhaps everything.

She had not intended to go on the defensive, but now she had to . . . that look on the Don's face warned her that she was pleading for her life.

'Juan Feliz has told you that he drove me into town the day we had those earth tremors,' she said, and she strove to keep her voice in control. 'And he's also told you that I didn't return with him to the hacienda but arrived home the following morning? And you think – you believe that I did something I ought to be ashamed of? But I didn't, *señor,* and that is the absolute truth. I went to the shops a-and then I started to stroll about among the houses with those charming old courtyards – all at once I felt the ground moving and scared out of my wits I ran into one of these courtyards and I tripped and struck my head – I was knocked out, *señor,* and these people in the house were kind enough to take care of me until the morning. It so rained that I couldn't get away until the break of day – and that's the truth—'

'Oh, it's true enough about the tremors, and the fact that you were hurt,' he said, and his eyes narrowed as they brushed across her forehead. 'You had facial bruises and they were seen by my servants – but what my servants haven't seen, or heard, just yet, is that you were with a young American all that night – ah, I see from the look on your face, *querida,* that you recall him. He works there, eh? Has fair hair and a rugged kind of face that appeal to girls, and charm of the easy-going variety. We met him once on the beach and you lied that time, as well. You pretended you didn't know him when all the time you did. Was it then that you arranged to meet again, as soon as my back was conveniently turned? Was it more pleasant in his arms, *mi vida,* than it was in mine?'

'I knew,' she cried out, straining to be free of these arms that felt like iron bands crushing breath and hope out of her, 'that you'd think what you are thinking! How do you know about Gil? Have you spies posted all over town? I – I noticed there was a slinky individual hanging around the morning after—'

'Really, the morning after being consoled by the so charming Señor Howard?'

'Oh – go to hell!' Persepha closed her eyes against the cruel dark look on his face and suddenly she didn't care two hoots if he took her neck in his hands and snapped her backbone. She waited coldly for the pain of it, for she knew him capable of the most utter ruthlessness, and who was there beyond these walls to care whether or not she was ever seen again. Gil Howard liked her well enough to aspire to an affair with her, but beyond that he felt no deep concern for her. He liked what the Don had already, her body and her hair and the cool golden looks that condemned her to be so wanted. Not for herself! Oh, never for the person she was at the heart and soul of her.

She flung back her head as if exposing her neck for his hands, and as she had thought they circled the slim pale column, dark against her skin, warm and threatening, his eyes shimmering down at her, intensely dark and dangerous.

'Yes, I should break your neck, *amiga,*' he said, in a soft and menacing voice. 'And if you wonder how I know about the American, then I will tell you, before you die first from sheer female curiosity. When I arrived home you did not come down to give me your warm and heartfelt welcome, so I went to my office to read any mail which had come to the hacienda during my absence. Sure enough there was a selection, and the most interesting of the lot was a grubby, ill-spelt, local letter, which out of sheer male curiosity I opened. It was from a certain person who used to be employed in my stables. In his bad, unstable hand he wrote to inform me that my wife was "sleeping" as he stated it, with an American named Gilberto Howard who worked in a gem store on the *avenida* in town. He had himself seen the two of you talking together near the store, and he followed you to Señor Howard's apartment not far from the *avenida*. You entered, he wrote, and he thought perhaps that you had gone there to look at some gems. But no, the following morning he saw you in the town square, riding off in a cab to the Hacienda Ruy, and he put "two together and made one."

'As he had this information,' the Don continued grimly, 'he thought I had better pay well for it unless I wished it to be known all over the region that I had a loose woman for a wife, who had put horns on my head, where they belonged to match my cloven pride. Well, *mi vida,* how do you think that hits a man just returned from a long and rather arduous trip? A pleasant welcome, eh? Better than a kiss any day, no?'

At the conclusion of his words Persepha could only gaze at him in sheer horror. 'Blackmail?' she gasped. 'By that man – the one I saw? That sallow little man with the bandit's moustache? Oh God, no wonder he looked at me with eyes like shotgun bores! He thought – and it isn't true, *señor*. I didn't sleep with Gil! I was on my way out of his apartment when the tremors came and threw me to the ground, where I struck my head. Gil looked after me – and what with the rain – I had no option but to stay at his place. He – he didn't touch me! I wouldn't have let him! I'm not that sort – you should know better than anyone that I – that I—'

'Oh, I know,' the Don said drily, and still holding his hands about her neck he bent his head and his lips closed on her lips, with those appealing words still upon them. Then he drew his mouth slowly away, and with narrowed eyes he studied her mouth, drawn slightly open like a sensuous flower against her creamy skin. 'Why did you go to his apartment, Persepha? He's a young and virile man, and he could be excused for thinking that a girl with honey in her eyes and a rather heartrending shape to her lips was a warm and generous creature. Don't tell me that he didn't flirt and that you weren't slightly flattered by his attentions? Were you running from him when you tripped and fell?'

'No,' she shook her head, even as a flush came into her cheeks at the way he had said "a warm and generous creature" as if in reality she was as cold and ungiving as the statue she had claimed to be. 'I'm not going to let Gil be blamed for any of this. He was kind and good to me. He bathed my head and behaved like a perfect gentleman.'

'I see.' The Don's expression was sardonic. 'He caught the chill blowing off the ice maiden and retreated before he developed frostbite. It takes a brave man, *querida*, that you will admit!'

She smiled just a little as she saw the ironic humour seeping back into his eyes. 'But what are you going to do about that nasty letter – I suppose it's from that groom you threw out of your stables? He had to find some way to get back at you, and he's trying to do it through me?'

'Exactly.' The Don drew his hands away from her as a white-coated manservant came along the terrace carrying a tray of drinks, which the Don had presumably ordered to be brought to them. They were set down on the terrace table, set at an angle that overlooked the gorge, and as the Don began to pour the drinks Persepha sat down again, rather glad to on account of her rather shaky legs. It had come as a shock that the Don had received a blackmail letter, and one that couldn't be completely proved as untrue. She had spent the night with Gil Howard, and though with entire innocence, it couldn't look anything but the usual sort of affair, conducted while her husband was absent on business.

'You will have sangria?' The Don's voice broke in on her distressed reflections, and when she glanced at the tray on the table she saw the tall pitcher of ruby-coloured sangria, a very Spanish drink concocted of wine, cognac, sections of fruit, sparkling ice, cinnamon and soda-water. It was a delicious drink on a hot day, and looked very inviting there in the cut-glass pitcher.

'Please,' she said, and realized how dry was her throat, as if she had been very close to a scorching flame and might have been far more seared than had been the case. Her lashes quivered, screening her eyes as they dwelt upon her husband. He had had every right to be furious about that letter, but now his face was quite impassive as he poured her drink and made a *pisco sour* for himself. That she had betrayed him he had not believed for an instant, though to frighten her a little he had pretended to play the outraged husband.

She was caught looking at him as he brought the tall glass of sangria to her and placed it in her hand. 'That will help steady your shaken nerves, *chica*,' he drawled, taking the cane chair beside her and stretching his long legs in an attitude of relaxation.

'*Gracias*,' she said, taking a long sip at the cool and delectable drink. 'But what are you going to do, *señor*? You can't just ignore the letter!'

'No,' he agreed, taking a slow pull at his own drink. 'I shall have to see the nasty-minded *hombre* and threaten him with jail. As it happens I know one or two things about him, and I also know the local police inspector very well. I don't think our *bandito* will get very far with his accusations.'

'But gossip can hurt,' she pointed out, and she flicked a quick look over the Don's proud dark face. 'Some people are going to believe what he tells them, and he's bound to if you refuse to give him money—'

'He gets not a penny from me,' the Don said curtly. 'When you pay a blackmail threat you admit guilt, and you have assured me that you aren't guilty of an indiscretion. I should hate to think that I had misjudged you after all, *querida*, and you were not so intrinsically virtuous that even a husband feels he is raping you each time he takes you in his arms. It isn't a pretty word, is it? But to the point.'

'I – I can't help it if I—'

'*Mi vida*, we have gone over this ground so often that turnips will soon start to grow in it. You hate me! Correct? You feel you were married against your will, and therefore I must always have you against your will. It might shake the patience of a saint, and my disposition is a trifle more satanic, eh? How is your sangria, sweet and cool?'

'Just right,' she said, and knew that he was flicking at her own disposition. 'How was the Argentine? Did you enjoy being there?'

'I did a lot of riding. Those horses trained by the gauchos are wonderful creatures, and I have purchased a mare and her foal for you. Lovely animals, who are being shipped to Mexico and should arrive in a few weeks.'

Weeks! Her heart seemed to turn over. He spoke as if no matter what the private situation was between them, it would go on, and on.

'What's the matter?' he asked, as if he had sensed rather than seen that turning of her heart. 'You like to ride, and you will have the sole care of these two superb animals. Dark as silk, *amiga*. They will pay a compliment to your fairness – and may I say that you are looking very delectable in that Latin-style dress, with the frill framing your slim legs.'

As his voice deepened, and his dark eyes stole from her ankles to her knees, and from her knees to her neck, Persepha had to fight not to jump to her feet and flee from his nearness. She had wild visions of being subjected to his ardency after ten days' celibacy, for curiously enough she no more believed that the Don had spent any of his passion in other arms than she had found consolation in Gil Howard's embrace. She knew with her deepest instincts that the Don still desired her in a way that sent the blood rushing through her veins, so that her heart beat wildly and a sensation almost of faintness stole over her.

She closed her hands tightly about the sangria glass, as if only by holding on to its cool firmness could she stop herself from leaping to her feet in a panic that would result in a dizzy collapse. She felt so odd, as if seeing him again, and hearing of the blackmail attempt, had combined to make a weak fool of her, so that she wouldn't be able to fight him with her usual show of spirit if he should sweep her into his arms and take her to that dim, cool, high-ceilinged room of his, where the air was tinged with that exotic tobacco he smoked, and where the silence was as deep as the fur that pelted his great couch ... like the couch of a barbarian.

'Don't worry,' he said, flicking his lighter at the cheroot he had just placed between his teeth. 'It's enough for now that I can look at you, so relax, *chica*. I am about to smoke not to act the ardent lover, and in truth your frigid dislike of me and my touch is enough to boil my blood, or to chill it, according to my mood. We re-enact the story of Lucrezia each time we meet, if only on the stairs.'

He emitted smoke in two decisive streams from his nostrils, and let his dark head rest against the tangerine cushion of his chair. He had removed his jacket before coming to the terrace and he wore a silk, brown-striped shirt that was only a shade or two darker than his skin. He lifted his hand and pulled loose his cream tie, and Persepha wondered why the casual actions of other men became tinged with a sensual danger whenever the Don performed them. He had only to walk into a room and its atmosphere became charged with tension, as if some magnetic force in him made the very air alive with potency and the promise of excitement.

It occurred to Persepha that as a boy he must have been as wild and unpredictable as any of the blooded stock running so arrogantly on the grasslands of his vast estate, sleekly muscled creatures that were cross-bred with some of the finest stock from other Latin countries. Had he been a source of anxiety to those parents about whom he never spoke? The turbulent heir to the Hacienda Ruy and its holdings, whom his mother had named after the Devil himself, seeing in the baby as he lay in her arms the dark-devil eyes looking up at her.

Had that mother of his passed on to him her ironic sense of humour? Had she been wild and beautiful and proud to have a son who was no saint? Persepha thought it possible, for she had been in this house long enough to have learned from Carmenteira and the maids that they admired beyond anything else a man who was unafraid to be a man. It seemed bred into the bones of Latin women, the liking for domination, and the ability to forgive a man anything but his indifference. They saw in her a woman who fought against being dominated by a Spaniard, and despite his seeming indifference to those threats of scandal made in that letter from his one-time stablehand, Persepha knew that it went against the deep hard grain of him to have it even hinted that he couldn't hold completely the reins on the spirited bride he had brought from England to share his life. His Mexican household would be even more suspicious of her ... they would say that there was no smoke without a bit of flame, and no smoke to blow in this direction if someone hadn't fanned it.

She sighed at the complex pattern of her life here in Mexico; all that old simplicity of days planned ahead for her by Marcus gone never to return.

She felt out of her depth, a secure hand withdrawn and replaced by one that either bruised or caressed, but never held hers with friendship.

The Don regarded her with lazy, all-seeing eyes; those of a master and tamer, admiring of his tigress but determined to take the edge off her claws, one way or the other; resolved to turn her bite into a kiss before he finally tired of her and turned his attentions elsewhere. He was thirty-six and had married at what Mexicans considered a mature age, but Persepha was quite certain there had been a number of women in his life, even if there had been only one perfect love. She was an interlude, exciting him by her difference to those other women, and by her indifference to him, but none of it could last if love was not its driving force. She had either to resign herself to a loveless future with this man, or she used some kind of guile to obtain those all-important documents in his desk that would ensure that she got across the Mexican border into the United States.

Gil Howard would help her. He wasn't a dog in the manger who ignored a bone just because he had not been allowed to get his teeth into it.

Then she gave almost a bone-jarring start as the Don leaned forward and laid dark fingers on her wrist. 'Your eyes are filled with conflict,' he said, quietly. 'Your mind is never at rest, and your heart is never content. You treat the hacienda like a cage, and you see me always with a whip in my hand. Will you never be happy here, *mi vida?*'

'Never,' she rejoined, the word a reflex, as the swift withdrawal of her hand was from that touch of warm hard fingertips. 'I'm too English to ever put down roots in your sun-hardened soil, *señor*. I wonder you hold on to someone whom your Mexicans regard as alien and reserved and passionless – wouldn't you be happier with a Latin wife, who would revel in your domination and your – your—'

'Can't you bring yourself to say it?' he taunted her. 'It's just a simple four-letter word.'

'Lust,' she gritted, through her very teeth, glaring into his dark mocking face and trembling slightly as his hand deliberately touched the upper part of her leg through the chiffon of her dress, stroking her as he might a little cat.

He smiled, showing his bone-white teeth. 'I have a surprise to show you after lunch, *chica*. A memento, let us say, which I brought with me from South America. I flew to Lima for a couple of days and my surprise comes from there. You may be – intrigued. Who knows, especially with a woman as unpredictable as you. So soft to touch, so hard to know.'

His fingertips slid away from her, leaving their pressure like a brand through the thin material of her dress; more telling than any bruise, really, that caress that was a mark of his possession.

'I think I should like to have lunch up here,' he said, stubbing his cheroot. 'Would you be so good as to do the ordering, Persepha, while I go and shower and change my clothes. I have been travelling in these and I feel the need to freshen up. Tell Orazio that I fancy steak for lunch, with perhaps musk-melon to commence with, a bottle of red Cadiz wine, and cheese – rich, ripe Spanish cheese with olives.'

'Yes, master,' she murmured, but when his eyes narrowed and his lashes made them gleam at her with mocking menace, Persepha leapt to her feet and hastened from his side, the frill of her dress flying up around her slim pale legs as she ran from him, half like a panicky adolescent, and half a woman with a turbulent knowledge of the danger and desire that could leap like a flame in that lean and supple male body, which was so swift and lethal in pursuit of its prey.

Reaching the outer staircase that twisted down to the courtyard she felt safe enough to fling him a last word. 'Onions with the steak, or not, *señor*?'

'Onions,' he said mockingly. 'Lashings of them, for the day is long when the moon rises late.'

Her heart tripped as she ran down the iron-grilled staircase ... the white-gold moon through those enormous windows, and dark shadow falling across her on that barbaric couch. She ran, pursued by his laughter.

The Don came to lunch on the terrace clad in a maroon silk shirt and narrow black trousers, looking as if he had revelled in an ice-cold shower, his hair still agleam from the water.

After seeing the chef, Persepha had changed her own dress, replacing its inviting femininity with a prim shirt and slacks with wide bottoms, sailor fashion, blue as the sky. She had combed out her hair and tied it with a shoelace, and she had cleaned all the lipstick from her mouth. She hoped she looked a passable schoolgirl, and when the Don quirked an eyebrow as he shook out his table-napkin, she felt she had succeeded.

'You look very sedate all of a sudden.' He quizzed her white shirt with its Peter Pan collar and cuffs. 'My dear, I don't need to be clairvoyant is order to read your transparent mind. I imagine the boyish apparel is meant to cool my husbandly ardour, but the only thing that might render that slim body of yours less enticing is a suit of Spanish armour. Have you ever seen any of the samples we have in one of the rooms in the older wing of the hacienda? Once inside a suit like that and only a mouse could penetrate to bother you.'

'You're very amusing, señor.' She tried to look casual as she chewed a slim stick of celery. 'I suppose you think I'd scream at a mouse?'

'No, only at a husband, funnily enough.' He shook a little sugar on his melon and started to eat with relish, and Persepha noticed throughout lunch that he had about him a buoyed-up air, as if he had something up his sleeve that was giving him a secret sort of pleasure. But he chose not to speak about it, and she supposed it had something to do with the surprise he had waiting for her after lunch.

'Excellent steak,' he said. 'No matter how well prepared the food in any other house, there really is no place like home for what a man truly enjoys. And these onions are cooked to perfection – more wine, Persepha?'

For some reason she thought she was going to need it and held out her wine glass to him. 'Just a little, señor, please.'

'Good wine, eh? I have a vineyard in Spain, did you know that? One day, chica, we must go and see the old country together.'

'Oh, I've been to Spain,' she said airily. 'Marcus took me a couple of years ago.'

'Going with your guardian and going with me are two different things,' he drawled, watching her over the rim of his glass as he took a long sip at his wine. 'With me you will see the real Spain, the one that lies enclosed from the casual visitor. I have some relatives scattered along the Iberian coast, and you have no idea how strangely romantic and filled with *saudade* are their walled court-yards.'

'*Saudade*?' she murmured, taking notice of his dismissal of her holiday in Spain with Marcus, which would strike him as a skimming of the surface of the Spanish way of life. 'What exactly does that word imply? Like a number of Spanish words it seems to have layers of meaning.'

'Just as we Spaniards have.' He gave a slight shrug, as if aware that she wouldn't care about that. 'The word can only be translated as nostalgia, dreams, the misty recol-lection of a memory that seems more to be desired than what we grasp in our two hands. Reality is the hot sun; *saudade* is the cool light of the moon. As moonlight can deceive, so can memory, and we have to beware not to live in the past. For the Spaniard, and indeed for others, there is in *saudade* a sublime sort of agony and ecstasy. If it were absent, unfelt, romance would lose its edge and its fascination.'

'Romance?' she echoed, staring at him, her fork sus-pended with a small wedge of steak impaled. 'I should never have thought that you believed in something so – so ephemeral and removed from the basic realities. You just don't strike me as a romantic person.'

'Which just shows, *querida*, that you have never really taken the trouble to know me.'

'No,' she shook her head and was about to argue fiercely with him, from her point of view, her knowledge of him, when she remembered that silver-framed photo-graph in his bedroom chest. *Saudade*, for a woman long dead. A memory of moonlight, of rose-coloured silk, and hair like the shadows of night. The words died on Per-sepha's lips. He was right, of course, she didn't really know the inner person that he was, for all he gave to her was the passion of his lean and splendid body; if he had

162

any more heart to give, then he probably saved it for the child she might give him. She believed he would love a child with more than the satisfaction of a man of possessions who required an heir; she had seen him with the children of Juan Feliz and some of the other members of his staff, and if there was a ruthless side to him, inherited from the past, there was also the Latin affection for the very young: a protectiveness she had been aware of even in her torment at being the person closest to his body and furthest from his heart.

'You were about to say?' He quirked an eyebrow, but his eyes knew well enough the words she had bitten back. 'That I am hard like nails and could never feel this moonlight and magic of the soul? Ah well, perhaps you are right. The soul is an elusive part of us, and when I look at you, seated there with the sun slanting on your lovely hair, it is the male side of me which reaps the real pleasure. How your lashes flutter when I speak of the way you look. After two months of marriage are you still shy of me?'

'It would probably take years for me not to be,' she rejoined. 'You have a way of looking – a way of speaking – they're not what I've been used to.'

'I should hope not!' He frowned slightly, though his eyes were mocking. 'To live with an English guardian, and to live with a Spanish husband, are two entirely different things.'

'Yes,' she agreed. 'He guarded me, but you possess me. He wandered with me in the pleasant ways of the mind, but you aren't interested in my mind, are you, *señor*?'

'Not to the exclusion of your delightful person, *mi vida*. I'd be a poor sort of man if I married such as you merely to discuss with you the excellence of good books and paintings. Was that what you hoped for? Not the natural state of wedlock, but the unnatural state of a husband locked out of your bedroom? Did you imagine when we met in England that because I was sixteen years your senior I would behave as if I were sixty years older?'

'I – I didn't even think about it.' She lowered her gaze, for to speak of these matters always made her feel on edge – restless. 'I was in a state of shock and you knew it, *señor*, and took advantage of it. I'd never have married you if I'd had time to consider your proposal – were you being completely honest when you said that Marcus approved of you as my – my husband?'

'I have my vices,' he said crisply, 'and strangely enough, I have my virtues, and one of them is that I never tell black lies, only white ones. I saw you at Stonehill and I – desired you. I asked your guardian for your hand in marriage, and he said that he would tell you on the way home from that party of his desire that you consider my proposal. He knew that I had land and a fine home, and he knew that if he died his own land and his own house would pass into the hands of a nephew. He told me of this, and in all fairness to the memory you have of him, it was this consideration that was uppermost in his mind. That you be provided for in the sudden event of his demise. He asked me—'

The Don paused and toyed with a knife. 'He requested that I be good to you. He warned me that you had been sheltered rather more than most English girls are these days.'

'But you – you chose to ignore that warning,' she said quietly.

'Did I?' He slung down the knife and the blade glittered like his eyes as the sun caught it. 'Your guardian was remiss in telling me that you also had a sharp little tongue and a tendency to argue with a man, and I was not used to that. I found you less than the little angel you appeared to be, and I treated you accordingly. I am but a man. Don Devil, eh? I believe that is your name for me?'

'I suppose you heard that from Carmenteira?' There was colour high on Persepha's cheekbones and little flickers of gold in her eyes, and she knew the Don was staring at her through his diabolical lashes. 'She potters about in my bedroom and pesters me, and no doubt comes to you with her tales. No one really approves of me. They all feel that I'm a let-down with my English looks and ways, and it's obvious they would have preferred a Latin mistress. *Señor*, why on earth didn't you marry a girl of your own race?'

'Because I married you,' he said harshly.

'And from the sound of your voice you're as sorry about it as I am,' she flung back at him.

'Really?' said a voice which seemed to come from out of the blue. 'Is this the way you two behave when you are alone together?'

In unison Persepha and the Don looked in the direction of the voice. '*Madrecita!*' he exclaimed, and pushed back his chair and was quickly on his feet. 'So you have found us out, eh?' He gave a laugh that was more disconcerted than amused. 'Discovered that when alone we don't bill and coo like lovebirds.'

'Diabo, put lovebirds in a cage together and they will peck each other to death,' said the small, beautifully coiffured, darkly clad woman who had appeared on the terrace in the midst of their quarrel.

Persepha could only stare at her, for the Don had called her grandmother, and she had believed that all his close relations were lost to him. Was this perfect figurine of an old lady the surprise he had spoken about? Persepha realized that if the woman had been in the car when it arrived she would not have seen her, for she had turned away when the Don had so mockingly bowed to her. She had gone to the other end of the terrace in order to regain her breath, her composure, and the courage to face him when he came to her after being away from her.

It came as a shock to meet this close relative of his, who having heard their duel of words would not be persuaded that they were madly in love with each other.

'*Madrecita,*' he said drily, 'come and meet my wife, the girl about whom you expressed doubts because she is English. You said, did you not, that it would be salt and pepper clashing together in the same pot?'

'*Si*, Diabo, I did say so.' The small and noble-looking woman kept her gaze fixed upon Persepha as she spoke to her grandson. Her eyes seemed not to miss a detail of the English features, and the way the slim, ringed fingers gripped the edge of the table. 'You are very charming, my child, and now that I do see you I can understand why Diabo allowed Spanish good sense to be swept from his mind. Salt and pepper don't really mix, but I imagine they can produce an interesting flavour. Come, you may kiss me!'

Persepha came round the table to the Don's grandmother and bending her head she pressed a kiss to the soft, powdered cheek. 'I – I'm happy to know you, *señora,*' she said shyly. 'I had no idea – Don Diablo said not a word about bringing you to the hacienda.'

'I imagine he wanted to give you a surprise.' The *senora* smiled, with a little touch of wickedness, as she sat down in the chair which her grandson drew out for her. 'I also imagine that he wanted to surprise me. He said you were young, fair, and inexperienced. He forbore to mention that you are extremely beautiful – my child, do be seated yourself, for you seem to be very shaken.'

'I – I am,' Persepha admitted, and now she cast a look

at her husband's face. It was impassive, giving nothing away. 'Oh, did he say—?' she wanted to cry out. 'Did he tell you why he married me?'

'Sit down, Persepha.' His hand pressed her down into her chair, and in front of his grandmother his hand didn't grip and linger, but it drew away and left her with the strangest, wildest inclination to reach out and pull it back to her person.

CHAPTER NINE

THE day that had passed had been a strange one, for after being introduced to the Señora Joaquina Calhariz, and after making polite and rather stilted conversation with her, Persepha had been left alone while the Don and his grandmother went off arm-in-arm for a tour of the hacienda which she had not seen for several years.

She was the Don's maternal grandmother, and when Carmenteira had spoken of the passing of her own mistress she had meant the paternal grandmother of Don Diablo. Persepha just hadn't dreamed that far away in the city of Lima there dwelt this charming but slightly aloof woman who had actually known him from a boy, and who could call him Diabo with an affectionate ease and tuck her arm within his as they went together to speak with his Mexican people.

The three of them had dined together last night, and then the *señora* had pleaded fatigue and the Don had escorted her to her bedroom suite, where her personal maid was waiting to assist her to bed. Persepha had lingered in the *sala*, but strangely enough the Don had not returned to her, and when she had gone to bed, taut with nerves because she had expected him, he had let the night pass without disturbing her.

Now it was morning and Persepha wandered alone through the dew-fragrant courts and gardens, breathing the glorious air, so untouched by the day because it was still very early.

She had not slept deeply, and several times had started awake, as if on thorns that suddenly the adjoining door was going to swing open to admit the Don. She had drifted off at last and awoken almost with the dawn, and at the call of the birds she had quickly washed and dressed and sped down to be alone with the flowers and the *reinatas* and the dragonflies that reminded her of the brooch that might assist her to fly away from this place that could never be her paradise.

Her gaze wandered over vines pearly with dewdrops, clusters of lilies with their golden calyxes, and a zephyr of colour winging through the morning sunlight that was delicious because it had not yet expanded into that brilliant ball that bounced its rays on the helplessly exposed earth.

The butterfly hung upon a petal, quivering there, intoxicated by the nectar that it drank in like wine, and Persepha stood very still so as not to disturb the delicate thing until it was ready to take wing and to fly out of reach.

And it was then that she heard bells coming from the direction of the chapel, so close that they drew Persepha, making her start, making her disturb the butterfly though she hadn't meant to. It flew ahead of her, its pale wings tipped with flame, and it seemed to guide her to the side entrance of the chapel among the trees, which stood partly open, so that she could see inside.

A hand clenched against her heart, for the Don was there, standing before the Madonna, and there were candles burning, and a mass of white roses were spread upon the altar. The proud dark head of the man was bent as if he prayed, and Persepha knew that he was totally unaware that she watched him in bated silence for several minutes. She seemed held to the spot by chains around her ankles; she couldn't move and just had to stand there and let her eyes wander over this stranger whom she had thought of as the total infidel: a man who took but who never relied on prayer to give him the things that he wanted.

At last she could move and she turned silently away and slipped like a shadow among the trees, until she reached the patio where she took breakfast since he had been away. She sat down in one of the fan-backed chairs to await the young maid with her *café con leche*. Tea was always taken to her bedroom, and it would be there now, growing cold beside her bed in which she had tossed so much that it looked as if a hurricane had passed over it. She knew what the maid would surmise, young Mafalda with whom she often had a laugh and a joke. The maids were earthy creatures, and as Don Diablo had once said to her, she wasn't averse to a joke.

She bit her lip and reached for a tea-rose that was opening its cup as the sun grew warmer. She had hold of it when she winced and saw a bead of blood on her finger. She put the finger to her lips, and wondered why it was that thorns had to grow among roses to cause pain, just as the problems of life could be so piercing.

Mafalda would hint in the kitchen that the *señor hidalgo* was more than delighted to be home with his bride!

Persepha stared at the blood on her finger . . . why had he suddenly let the door remain closed between them? She had felt instinctively that he had not been with another woman while in South America, yet after ten days he had chosen to ignore her. Could it be that he felt reserved with his grandmother in the house? It was a possibility, yet not one that Persepha found convincing.

She visualized him once again at the altar of the little chapel, and she seemed to breathe again the powerful perfume of the roses. Pale like a woman's skin . . . roses for remembrance . . . and for love.

She caught her breath, for sharper, more real, was the

possibility that his grandmother's presence here had brought back talk, and memories, of that lovely Latin woman whose death he had taken so hard. Was that why he had not been able to face her last night, because he and the *señora* had talked of that other woman, recalling her presence at the hacienda, her beauty and her laughing, flirtatious eyes above the frilled edge of a lace fan.

His *madrecita,* like everyone else, could not approve his choice of an English wife. The old lady had been polite, but not really friendly, and Persepha's teeth bit upon her own finger as she saw ahead of her days in which she was under scrutiny by his grandmother, her every action watched and commented upon. Her clothes studied, and her attitude towards the Don himself criticized for its lack of emotional warmth which a Latin bride would have shown him.

'I can't stand it!' Persepha muttered the words to herself. 'I shall have to get away!'

Then she sensed rather than saw another presence on the patio, and pulling herself together she stood up and turned casually to face whoever stood there in the shade of a madrone tree.

She had half expected to see the Don, but instead his grandmother had risen early and had appeared on the patio in that silent, unnerving way of Latin people, as if they walked as they danced, with an animal grace that made their feet seem in tune with the very earth.

'*Buenas dias*, my child.' The voice was richly sweet and cool, and there was a rustle of silk, and a sparkle of diamonds in a harp-shaped brooch as the *señora* came gliding across the softly coloured tiles of the patio, elegant in an old-fashioned style, both in her dress and her manner. As she approached and was quite plainly going to take the opportunity to speak to her grandson's wife alone, it took all of Persepha's courage to stand there and not obey her impulse to dash indoors out of the way of this Spanish woman who had overheard her say to the Don that she was sorry she had ever married him.

Having been brought all the way to the Hacienda Ruy to meet her grandson's bride, it was hardly the sort of thing she would have hoped to hear. Persepha pushed her hands deep into the pockets of her cabin-boy pants as the Señora Joaquina Calhariz ran her Latin eyes over the pants, which emphasized the slimness of Persepha's figure, which had none of the voluptuous roundness of hip that was apparent in young Mexican women.

'Good morning, *señora*.' Persepha spoke politely in English, though in the weeks she had been here she had acquired a fluency with the Spanish language which she kept mainly for use when speaking with the staff. Whenever the Don spoke to her in his language, she invariably answered him in English, as if asserting her claim that she would never be anything else but a woman who lived here against her will. But he knew well enough that already she could speak excellent Spanish; more than once he had strolled into her bedroom while she was in conversation with Mafalda or Becke, a pair of Mexican sisters who quarrelled endlessly about their boy-friends. They had begun to ask her advice about these boy-friends, as if as a married woman she had some insight into love that they didn't have as yet, and she knew how much it amused the Don that the Mexican girls should ask her such frank and outrageous questions. He'd quirk that devilish black brow of his as he lounged against the bedpost with a cup of coffee, and tell her not to be shy but to go ahead with her advice bureau. She knew that the two maids found him the epitome of Spanish *muy hombre,* and they'd giggle like a pair of fools when he was in the room, and deliberately flutter their long Latin eyelashes at him. They were both exceedingly pretty, and almost alike as a pair of pins except that Becke had a velvety mole beside her upper lip. In any other household, Persepha couldn't help but realize, such come-hither boldness from such girls would have resulted in the master straying in their direction. But she had seen the Don look amused by them and nothing more. He had a curious aloofness when it came to other women, and Persepha felt sure she knew the reason.

'I had hoped,' said the Don's grandmother, 'that you and I could have a conversation together. When the girl Becke told me that you were probably down here on the patio awaiting your breakfast, I decided to join you. I don't usually rise so early, so you must consider yourself of much interest to an old woman who likes to lounge in bed with her newspaper.'

'It was kind of you to join me,' Persepha still couldn't relax with this woman who must find her so hard to accept as the wife of a grandson she obviously adored. An English girl with hair that caught the sunlight, who wore boyish pants, and didn't cling to Don Diablo as if he were her staff and her comfort. She drew out a chair for the *señora* at the patio table, who sat down carefully, sighing a little as the elderly do, and revealing a tiny elegant foot beneath the long hem of her dress.

'My old bones ache a little after that long journey yesterday,' she said. 'But I just had to come and meet you, my child. And please sit down so that I can see you without having to look up at you – you are a tall girl compared to Latin girls, though it is not so noticeable when you stand beside Diabo. Every so often a man of his build is born into the Ezreldo Ruy family, for long ago Aztec blood mingled with Ezreldo blood, and the nobles of that time were tall, so that they had authority over their people. You find in him the smouldering fire of the absolute Latin, eh?'

'I – I find him different from any Englishman,' said Persepha, seating herself at the other side of the circular table, which was set against a bank of margaritas and huge roses, tall gladioli and plumy ferns; it was a setting she normally found attractive and relaxing, but not with the *señora*'s shrewd eyes upon her, taking in her skin, her features, her slim neck running into the open collar of her white shirt.

'If he is so different, why did you marry him?' The question was so direct that Persepha knew in an instant that the Don had not told his grandmother the full facts of their relationship. The *señora* thought they had met and courted in the normal way, and Persepha knew an instant, flaring desire to fling the bald facts across the table. And then she hesitated, for this woman was old and she had only memory and illusion to live upon. She loved the Don, for he was of her blood and she had held him in her arms when he was born. She had unbreakable ties with him; a bond of sympathy and understanding that no English girl could hope to break.

And Persepha had no real wish to break it . . . love was too elusive and too precious to be treated to the acid of her own disillusion.

'It just happened,' she said hesitantly. 'We met and married very quickly—'

'And are you now repenting at leisure?' the *señora* asked dryly. 'I'd be an old fool if I thought it an ideal marriage which Diabo has undertaken, but he was always a man for a challenge, and as he has grown into maturity I have known that he would not settle for the placidity of life with a woman who would give him a clutch of babies but never an argument. You are like the *grenadilla,* lovely on the outside, but starchy and filled with pips that stick in a man's teeth. I don't doubt that Diabo enjoys shaking some of the starch out of you, and tackling those pips with his strong white teeth.'

The *señora* smiled to herself, and then reached out to take hold of Persepha's gold-ringed hand. Her fingers were remarkably strong, like tiny, thin claws, the skin like ivory against Persepha's pale suntan. 'Was it Diabo's money that drew you to Mexico? The women of Europe can be very mercenary, as they can in the United States. They place the possession of worldly things before the gift of love – I find myself thinking that women of the North are losing rapidly what the women of the South still retain – the ability to give all to a man. Body, heart and spirit. They give the body, but coldly, and keep the heart in cold storage. Are you one of these women?'

'No! I'd never marry any man just for his money,' Persepha said, with heat. 'You have no right—'

'Oh, but I have, my child. I have the right of someone who loves Diabo and would like to see him made happy. He has not been a happy man, you know. Certain things happened some years ago that blighted his life for a while, and I came with him to Mexico in the hope of finding that at last the old sad memories had been buried, or carried away on the winds like the black seeds that give birth to twisted plants.' The tensile fingers gripped Persepha's. 'Does he ever speak to you of the past?'

'Never at any time,' Persepha admitted. 'But I know—'

'What do you know?' The *señora* stared into the hazel eyes that held so much emotional conflict, giving them a beauty that was curiously poignant, matched by the mouth that was shaped to express passion and temper and a dulcet pity.

'Carmenteira told me certain things – she has been here so many years that there are no secrets concealed from her. She let me into one or two, as was bound to happen. She resents me because I'm not a Latin, and I know about

175

the Don's unhappiness of six years ago. He married me, *señora,* but it's no use pretending that there aren't regrets on his side as well as mine. You heard what we said to each other yesterday.'

'So I did,' the *señora* admitted.

'I'm sorry if it came as a shock to you.'

'It really came as no surprise. As soon as Diabo told me you were English I knew that traditional enemies had met on the field of battle, and that it was going to take a high degree of love and tolerance for such a marriage to work.'

'And now you see that it isn't working.' Persepha lowered her glance and watched as a lizard skimmed across the sunlit tiles of the patio with the wing of a butterfly poking from its jaws. She gave a shiver . . . was it the same butterfly which had led her to the chapel, where she had seen the Don paying homage to a memory? Having lost heaven he settled for hell . . . it could be nothing else for either of them, not without love to heal the wounds of battle; to soothe away the sting of quick words spoken by two people with quick tempers. Love made fun of the fighting . . . but hate only left resentment and pain.

The lizard flickered out of sight among the ferns, there to feed on its delicate victim.

'Ah, here comes the girl with our breakfast,' said the *señora.* 'I have quite an appetite this morning. Usually I don't eat until mid-morning. *Chica,* what have you brought us?'

The girl smiled vividly at the Don's grandmother, and whisked off the snowy napkin to reveal a marvellous tortilla, rich with eggs, chopped ham and herbs, crisp at the edges, and served with country bread which had been freshly baked that morning. The aromatic smoke of the coffee came drifting from the spout of the silver pot, and the cream was thick in the jug.

'Everything looks delicious!' The *señora* brought her hands together in a pleased motion. 'No wonder, Persepha, you take breakfast on the patio if they treat you like this. A gesture of gratitude, eh, that they don't have to carry trays up and down the stairs as in the days—' The Don's grandmother broke off her words, and then lifted the lid of a little silver dish, disclosing fresh strawberries on a bed of orange slices. '*Es bueno*, who could wish for more?'

'It's usually apricots and rolls, and sometimes figs,' Persepha smiled. 'This is in your honour, *abuela*.'

'Will the *señor* be joining you for breakfast?' the girl asked, before departing with the empty tray, its contents having been laid upon the table.

'I don't think so – he may have gone riding.' Persepha swallowed a slight dryness from her throat. 'I saw him earlier and he was clad in his riding breeches and boots.'

As she spoke and lifted the silver pot, feeling the almost desperate need for coffee with cream, she saw him again in her mind, standing there in the chapel with a finger of sunlight across the shining tips of his boots that were never spurred, though his horses were high-couraged and took a lot of handling. That day long ago, when death had closed the eyes of the woman he loved, he had, according to Carmenteira, ridden his favourite horse to its last breath.

He would be riding now, Persepha knew it, galloping hard across the pampas on Satanas, his present favourite.

'Have coffee ready for him in the kitchen, Mafalda,' she said. 'I should imagine he'll be back in about an hour.'

'*Si, señora.* Enjoy your food.' The girl was gone with a

177

swirl of flared skirt, the sunlight catching blindingly on the surface of the silver tray as she swung it, careless and happy in her youth, not all that much younger than Persepha, who yet felt as if a weight of responsibility and decision rested on her own slight shoulders.

'You have an excellent mastery of Spanish,' remarked the *señora*, as she shook pepper on to her tortilla. 'Diabo has been teaching you?'

'Not deliberately. I gradually picked it up, and I knew a little before I came here. You take cream, *señora*?'

'*Gracias*. A while ago you called me *abuela* – grandmother. I would prefer that, for it sounds less formal. And what does Diabo call you? We Latins have a liking for diminutives, and you have a rather strange, long name. Not quite English, I think.'

'No, it's from mythology. I was named by my guardian who was something of a classical scholar when a young man. He meant to be a writer, and then found his talent lay elsewhere. He was a famous gambler – did the Don tell you?'

'He will confide in me gradually.' The *señora* tasted her breakfast and smiled her approval. 'As good as it looks. Now, what does he call you so that I may, with your consent, use the same name?'

'He has never shortened my name.' Persepha realized this with a sense of surprise. 'I do believe he rather likes it. Or perhaps the mythological story attached to it.'

'Which is?' The *señora* quirked an eyebrow and for an instant Persepha saw a resemblance in this woman to the man; shades of his ironic humour and his tendency to mock her when she was being too serious.

'I – I'm sure you know the story.' Persepha drank her coffee with desperate thirst. 'The dark lord of Hades took a bride and her name was Persephone. For half a year she was forced to share his world, and then she was permitted to go home to her family for the remainder of the year.'

'But I understand that you have no family – Persepha.' The smile had gone from the *señora*'s eyes. 'And I hope you don't plan to leave my grandson's world – he would only fetch you back.'

'Like a wife in purdah,' Persepha couldn't resist saying.

'Like a wife, not a foolish child. He doesn't shut you up and not allow you the freedom of his hacienda. You can go where you please, but there are men in this region who do treat their wives with far more harshness than Diabo would ever show any woman. He has his faults, but he has something beyond price when it comes to a woman – he actually likes the look and taste and feel of a woman, and he doesn't regard them merely as breeding machines. Are you aware of this, or are you too naïve to recognize a real man when you find yourself married to one?'

All at once her voice had sharpened and grown scornful, matching the look which she flung over Persepha's person. 'He said you were young, but I never dreamed you were infantile.'

'Th-that's unfair!' Persepha felt as if she had been slapped. 'I think I've taken it rather well, being dragged here to Mexico to be the wife of a high-placed, high-handed Don, who really wants me for only one thing—'

'Be proud of it.' The *sénora* snapped her fingers so her rings glittered and flashed fire in the sunlight that fell through the boughs of the tree shading the table.

'You say he doesn't regard a woman as a breeding machine, but that's all he wants from me – a child,' Persepha choked, having tears and a little too much pepper in her throat. 'A son to take over his precious estates and his herds of cattle and his stables of horses and his farms full of Mexican retainers and their parcels of children. It doesn't matter that he doesn't love me, for what has love

179

to do with the getting of a baby? It's enough that I arouse the animal in him—'

'Enough of that!' The *señora* flung down her cutlery with every vestige of the Don's own chilling anger. 'How dare you speak of my grandson in that manner – where did he find you, in the docks of some English port where the women use the language of men?'

Persepha flushed hotly . . . she hadn't meant to lose her temper or her dignity, but it was really too much that she be expected to play the lovelorn bride just to please a woman who was as basically contemptuous of her as everyone else she met here. Only the maids were friendly, and only because they couldn't take her seriously as their mistress. To them she was just the boudoir toy of the *señor hidalgo,* to whom all the staff went when anything important cropped up, such as an outbreak of fire in the kitchen, or a child falling off the stable gate. Mexicans were panicky, she had discovered, but to the master they ran rather than the mistress when accident befell them or their children.

She would never be the mistress here . . . and in blind haste she thrust back her chair and sprang to her feet. Her face was white, so that her eyes seemed over-large and a burning gold-brown colour, like pools of pain. 'I don't want a child from him,' she cried out. 'I'd sooner throw myself over a balcony than give birth to it!'

As her words rang out on the patio, a lean dark hand swept aside a curtain of plumbago and a tall figure, booted and breeched, stepped into view. That he had caught those wild, unhappy words was plain on his face. That they had struck him like a lash was apparent from the bitter twist to his mouth.

Persepha saw him from the corners of her eyes, and she ran in fear and fury from him and all that was part of him, making for the outer staircase that led up to the gallery, from whence she could reach her room. She meant to go, to insist on it, and with his grandmother in the house he couldn't hold her against her will. Neither of them could be that uncivilized . . . that cruel.

She reached the staircase and because she knew that the Don had caught her words, she feared that he would catch her and she ran in a wild terror up those stairs.

'Persepha!' Her name rang out behind her. 'Little fool, you will break your neck!'

She didn't pause, though her heart seemed to for a second. He was pursuing her, and if he once touched her . . . no, she cried the word, and fled him along the gallery, hearing the sudden thud of his boots on the tiles. She reached the arched entrance that led into the interior gallery, and she could feel the perspiration breaking through her pores, making her silk shirt cling to her, while her loosened hair whipped her neck and face as she cast one single glance behind her.

He looked as dark and terrible as Mars in pursuit of Rhea . . . an almost crazed look on his face as if he meant to punish her severely for what she had said . . . and what she had said was unforgivable, and a sob broke from her as she reached the door of her room and caught wildly at the handle. She dashed inside, but even as she slammed the door behind her, she had no sanctuary from him, for he would come through the connecting door from his own room and she'd be trapped in here with him and his justifiable anger.

Oh God, to say it to his grandmother! He would never forgive her for that . . . it had been like striking the old lady, whose remaining hopes on earth must be centred on seeing a great-grandson at the Hacienda Ruy, proof to her Spanish heart that the family would go on.

Persepha glanced round wildly . . . where could she go? Then she saw the doors standing open at the other end of the room, leading out to the balcony that overlooked the gorge. She'd be safer out there, for he wouldn't rant and rave under the close eye of heaven, and he might let her go before this hell of a marriage broke her heart, or he broke her neck.

She was at the glass doors and about to step on to the balcony when he thrust open the door from his room and appeared in the aperture like a figure of doom itself.

The look of him was too much for Persepha ... how was she ever going to reason with a man whose face expressed a sort of agony, as if only by hurting her could he assuage the pain and fury which he felt. She whirled and ran to the parapet of the balcony, looking herself like a vixen who had been hunted to the edge of her reason and had nowhere else to go. She clung there, crying out and gripping the stone, when his angry hands caught at her and wrung his name from her for the very first time. It was like the cry of a woman dying, or giving birth, and then all she saw in all the world was his dark face as he literally tore her from the parapet and swung her into his arms.

'That you won't do!' The words were thick, choked, as if with passion and tears. 'Not again will a woman do that in this house!'

And then he was carrying her back into the bedroom, and in a sudden helplessness she burst into tears and they were spilling down her face when he laid her on the bed, and laid himself across her body. 'Do you hate me so much?' he groaned. 'Would you throw yourself to the stones rather than live with me?'

She heard him, but she was too shaken, too distressed, to be able to make sense of what he said. She lay there, held to the bed by his hard frame and the grip of his arms, and she could feel him watching her, his eyes as dark as night with a storm at their centre. It was his silence, his stillness, which finally stilled her own weeping, and as the tears died away, the meaning in his words drifted back.

Throw herself to the stones? Over the balcony and all the way to the hard ground, to lie there broken and no longer aware of sunlight or moonlight; of hate or love.

'I wasn't ...' She shook her head. 'Not that ... I was afraid and there was nowhere else to go.'

'Afraid?' His face was so still, and yet his eyes seemed alive with a number of expressions ... the disbelief she recognized, and it was so incredible that he should think she had been going to throw herself off the balcony.

'Yes, you looked so furious over what I said – oh, why can't you let me go and be done with it? What kind of satisfaction does it give you to hold on to me when you know – it isn't that you're truly sadistic, but pride of possession is so deep in your bones, and you only want me so that I – I'll give you a baby—'

'Only for that?' The line of irony etched itself beside his mouth. 'My dear fool, if all I wanted from any woman was a child, then I'd do better by far to marry a fecund and affectionate Mexican girl, who would be happy to be pregnant every year for the next dozen years. Hell or heaven itself knows why I married you, but I won't have you so unhappy and afraid that you'll smash yourself on the stones of my courtyard ...'

As he said this a spasm of sheerest torment went across his face, and all at once his hand touched her face, curving itself to her cheek and her neck and drifting down to her shoulder, where it stayed itself. 'Once before in my life I have had to see a woman broken and bleeding down there, and I promise you, Persepha, that if you are so desperate to leave my house, then you shall leave.'

She heard him, but her heart didn't leap with the joy of relief ... the words that lingered, that beat in her brain, were those he had spoken before he had said that she might leave.

'Is that how she died?' Persepha almost whispered the words, for she was a little afraid of them, of speaking aloud of that someone who was sacred to him.

'Yes.' A deep sigh lifted his chest, and then as if he realized that his weight was crushing her, he drew away, and instantly her body felt cold, abandoned, and she had the strongest urge to grab at him and hold him close and hard again, so that nothing, not even a shadow, could come between them. The sensation was so acute it was a pain and her fingers gripped the lace bedcover, uncaring if they ripped it. She wanted him ... wanted Diablo, whether or not he loved her.

Suddenly she felt that she grew up and could face what had seemed impossible to endure ... suddenly she knew how hellishly he had suffered when that other woman had died in that awful way.

'How could she do it?' Persepha asked softly. 'How could she hurt you like that when she knew you loved her?'

'She knew I loved her, but she blamed me for Alvarado's death.' The words came jerkily, hesitantly, as if he had never thought to say them, least of all to her.

'You mean—' Persepha stared at his dark and tortured face. 'She loved your brother?'

'But of course.' His eyebrow twisted, not in the old quizzical way, but with a wry puzzlement. 'He was the son she loved best, even though I loved her so much. *Madre mia*, so charming and lovely, and so delighted always to see Alvarado in her own image. Slender, with her great eyes, and the easy way of going through life. He was her saint, I was her devil and her devil incarnate when Alvarado developed polio after he and I had gone out to the reef where a tiger shark had its hide. It had

184

come in close to the beach and taken the legs of a young fisherman, and it was Alvarado who challenged me to go with him to capture and kill the shark. Madre said I should have refused to go, and kept Alvarado from going. But he would have gone, nevertheless, and because I feared that the shark might attack him in the way it had that other young man, I went with him. We killed the brute, using an Indian sea-bow loaded with steel-headed darts, and afterwards there was a *fiesta* in town, with everyone celebrating the chase and the kill.'

The Don paused and his eyes dwelt with an unseeing sadness on Persepha, who lay there quietly, just looking, and listening intently to his every word. He had called the woman *madre mia* , and she had almost cried out with an ecstasy of relief. Without actually lying old Carmenteira had implied that the woman in the photograph had been his sweetheart . . . in truth she had been his mother.

'In those days it was a dirty sea and a beach fit only for scavengers, and there was polio on the outbreak at the time Alvarado and I swam there for well over two hours, hunting the shark. It was only a matter of days before he was attacked by the severest symptoms. An iron lung was rushed from Mexico City, but to no avail. My young and handsome brother, so delightful to know, and with so much to live for, choked to death with no ability left in his laughing lungs for them to draw breath. *Madre mia* never left his side and she had to watch him die in agony. Afterwards, in words that I shall never forget, she told me that she wished it had been me who had died. That I was a reincarnation of the Devil because I had taken Alvarado out into the sea to be tainted by all that foul water. I was too hard, too much an iron man, as my father had been, to ever fall victim to polio. But because Alvarado had been lighthearted and a joy to all eyes, he had been taken.'

Again a long and painful pause, and by this time Persepha was dying to hold him and comfort him; to show him that she no longer believed him to be entirely a devil ... only the kind of devil that circumstances had made him. A man who blamed himself for his mother's suicide.

'It happened,' he said, almost inaudibly, 'the evening of the funeral, just as the sun was dying, and no sun dies anywhere as it does here, in a sort of agony of flame and beauty. I heard her scream, and I was the first to find her. It happened six years ago, and the Hacienda Ruy was a house of shadows for a long time. Then one day I met a man named Charles Paget who showed me a miniature, and who requested that if ever I was in England I would ensure that his daughter was not in want or trouble. To me, when your guardian was no longer alive to care for you, you seemed in want and trouble, and you also seemed like the sunshine in my life again.'

He studied her hair, a tumbling mass of pale gold against the white lace, and his face was in conflict, the desire to treat her gently at war with that other emotion which up until now had always made of her a struggling victim rather than a willing participant in his passion.

But if all that he had to give was passion, she now loved him enough to accept it. Of her own accord Persepha leaned to him and pressed her lips to his hard cheek ... he was very still as he accepted the first voluntary caress she had ever given him, then he suddenly spoke, and his voice struck at her so harshly that she shrank away again.

'Don't give me pity! That's the last thing on earth that I want from you! Don't you know – have you not yet grown up enough to realize what I want from you?'

'I – I've always known,' she said, and she blinked hard, so as not to cry for him and for herself. 'It's just a four-letter word, isn't it, but it sticks in my throat.'

'It would.' He almost snarled at her. 'You've always

found it easy to cry "hate" at me, and that's why I've never lived for the false hope that you'd ever whisper that other word.'

'Whisper it?' She looked at him with bewildered eyes. 'Live in hope that I'd say it? But it's an ugly word—'

'Ugly?' He raked his eyes over her, and then a curious expression began to settle about his lips, until they almost seemed to be smiling. 'There are two words between a man and a woman that say everything or nothing, and they both begin with the letter L. So you think, *querida*, that I have only lusted after you, eh? Like some lout without feelings other than those of the animal? My foolish child, I have longed to give you heaven, but it seems that I have only given you hell, and though I hoped just before I left for South America that I had at last made you feel something of what I have felt, today has proved me very wrong.'

He sighed and dragged a hand down over his cheek. 'I shaved too rapidly this morning, but it was the anniversary of *madre mia*'s birthday and I wanted to take roses to the chapel – what is it, *chica*, why do you look at me like that?'

'I saw you, Diablo,' she said softly. 'In the chapel this morning, among the candles and roses. You seemed so – lonely. I – I don't want to go away if you'll be lonely – oh, please, don't flare up, and don't shout at me again.' And suddenly she couldn't bear it if he became angry with her, and blindly she reached for him and flung her arms about his neck and pressed herself against him. 'I – I don't pity you, *señor*, I only pity myself for the idiot I've been. That night before you left on your trip I thought – I believed that you wanted me to have your child. I thought that was all you cared about – but was it, Diablo? Was it only that?'

'Never, as the good *deus* is my witness!' Suddenly his

arms were so tightly bound around her that she almost lost her breath. 'I hoped to make you love me, *quer-idisma,* for having you, holding you, dragged the very heart out of me. I wanted never to let you go, and yet I felt that if I went away for a while, you might miss me. Did you, *querida?* Did you ever miss me for a single moment, as I missed you, seeing the sun on your hair in the play of morning light; seeing the candle-glow in your eyes when we dined together. I wanted to demand that you love me, but I knew I had to have some sort of patience – it is very hard, *chica,* for someone like me to have that kind of patience.'

She lay there very still in his arms, listening to his every word . . . then all of a sudden a quiver ran all through her and her hands tightened on his shoulders, pressing into his warm skin.

'You took,' she whispered, 'but you never told me that you – cared.'

'I was a fool.' His hand ran strong and loving down her soft mane of hair. 'I forgot you were little more than a girl and I took you for a woman – I thought to tell you with my body that I adored you, but instead I frightened you. Do I frighten you now? Do I – I demand to know!'

'No—' she gave a quivering laugh. 'Yes, and no, Diablo. Always you will bring my heart into my throat in a dozen different ways, but if I know that you love me, then anything will be bearable. Anything!'

'This?' He bent his head and slowly kissed her mouth. 'And this?'

The power and strength of his kisses shafted through her and as she twined her arms about his neck, holding him, a voice spoke from the doorway of the bedroom:

'Ah, once again I appear to have arrived at an inopportune moment.'

Husband and wife turned their heads in unison, and

they both smiled at the tiny, elegant figure by the door.

'*Madrecita*, do come in!' said the Don courteously.

'My dear Diabo,' she rejoined, 'I think I know when I should go out again.' The *señora* smiled at both of them, a sudden tenderness in her eyes. '*Adios* for now – I will see both of you – later.'

The bedroom door closed quietly behind her.

Did you miss our splendid Doctor/Nurse Series?

CHILDREN'S HOSPITAL
by Elizabeth Gilzean

Would Sister Sandra Lorraine and 'new broom' consultant Peter Donaldson ever come to understand each other?

HOSPITAL CORRIDORS
by Mary Burchell

Madeline was looking forward to her year in a big Montreal hospital. Would she be disappointed?

DOCTOR LUCY
by Barbara Allen

Lucy was through with love and intended to concentrate on her career—as she made clear to her chief, that clever surgeon Paul Brandon. .

BORNE ON THE WIND
by Marjorie Moore

Why was Duncan McRey so kind to his child patients and yet so harsh and unfriendly to Sister Jill Fernley?

A PROBLEM FOR DOCTOR BRETT
by Marjorie Norrell

Brett Hardy had two things to do before leaving St. Luke's Hospital—apologise to Sister Janet Morley, and then consult a marriage bureau . . .

SUCH FRAIL ARMOUR.
by Jane Arbor

Kathryn could have borne Adam Brand's hostility if she hadn't had to work alongside him all day and every day!

JUNGLE HOSPITAL
by Juliet Shore

A romantic story set in the jungle of Malaya.

THE HEART OF A HOSPITAL
by Anne Vinton

Would Sister Eve Ramsey's selfish sister manage to ruin her career?

35p net each

FREE!
Your copy of the Mills & Boon Catalogue —
'Happy Reading'

If you enjoyed reading this MILLS & BOON romance and would like to obtain details of other MILLS & BOON romances which are available, or if you are having difficulty in getting your TEN monthly paperbacks from your local bookshop, why not drop us a line and you will receive, by return and post free, the MILLS & BOON catalogue—*'Happy Reading'*.

Not only does it list nearly 400 MILLS & BOON romances, but it also features details of all future publications and special offers.

For those of you who can't wait to receive our catalogue we have listed over the page a selection of current titles. This list may include titles you have missed or had difficulty in obtaining from your usual stockist. Just tick your selection, fill in the coupon below and send the whole page to us with your remittance including postage and packing. We will despatch your order to you by return!

MILLS & BOON READER SERVICE, P.O. BOX 236, 14 Sanderstead Road, South Croydon, Surrey, CR2 OYG, England.

Please send me the free Mills & Boon catalogue ☐

Please send me the titles ticked ☐

I enclose £.................... (No. C.O.D.) Please add 5p per book—standard charge of 25p per order when you order five or more paperbacks. (15p per paperback if you live outside the U.K. & Europe).

Name.. Miss/Mrs

Address ....

City/Town ....

County/Country.....................Postal/Zip Code..................

XP75

Your Mills & Boon Selection!

☐ 001
THE BLACK CAMERON
Jean S. MacLeod

☐ 002
MY TENDER FURY
Margaret Malcolm

☐ 003
LOVE IS FOR EVER
Barbara Rowan

☐ 004
WHO LOVES BELIEVES
Elizabeth Hoy

☐ 005
SECRET HEIRESS
Eleanor Farnes

☐ 006
GREENFINGERS FARM
Joyce Dingwell

☐ 007
THE THIRD UNCLE
Sara Seale

☐ 008
MARRY A STRANGER
Susan Barrie

☐ 104
THE GIRL AT WHITE DRIFT
Rosalind Brett

☐ 130
THE AFFAIR IN TANGIER
Kathryn Blair

☐ 132
RIVER NURSE
Joyce Dingwell

☐ 133
INHERIT MY HEART
Mary Burchell

☐ 156
A CASE OF HEART TROUBLE
Susan Barrie

☐ 253
MISS MIRANDA'S WALK
Betty Beaty

☐ 255
PARADISE ISLAND
Hilary Wilde

☐ 269
A PLACE CALLED PARADISE
Essie Summers

☐ 283
ISLE OF SONG
Hilary Wilde

☐ 287
THE PRIDE YOU TRAMPLED
Juliet Armstrong

☐ 288
WINTERSBRIDE
Sara Seale

☐ 293
HOTEL BY THE LOCH
Iris Danbury

☐ 298
QUEEN'S COUNSEL
Alex Stuart

☐ 300
HOTEL SOUTHERLY
Joyce Dingwell

☐ 302
BELOVED SPARROW
Henrietta Reid

☐ 304
THE MASTER OF
NORMANHURST
Margaret Malcolm

☐ 307
THE DREAM AND THE
DANCER
Eleanor Farnes

All priced at 25p net

Please tick the titles you require and use the handy order form overleaf for your requirements.